Strange Clouds
A Melanated Fantasy Joint, Book I

To Arnilla

Thank you so much for your love & support. Your super powers are needed in the world ✿

Mad Love,
Cheketa

Printed and bound in the United States of America

First Edition

978-0692715130

To my husband, Will. Without your endless support, Strange Clouds would not have been possible. Thank you for encouraging me to write this thing "Che Style". This one is for you!

Namaste.

I give thanks and honor to the Most High, the Most Divine, The Universe and all that is meant for my highest good. I would also like to thank my husband, Will, for his continuous support and for being my number one fan. Thank you, Gary Struggs, for your contribution to Raysean's freestyle borrowed from the first verse of your song, *I Can Tell You The Game.* Shout out to my daughters, Keesha and Shy; sisters, Charlie and Gwen; my brother, Tony; and cousins, Theresa, Vernessa, Micah, and Neema for being my first readers, for inspiring me to believe in my artistry, and to see it into fruition.

I need to give a huge thanks to Aletha Fields and Khalilah Collins for being my editing eyes. I love you guys to life! Super duper thanks to the "Illest Strator", Kevlen Goodner, for the amazing artwork. Can't wait to get started on the comic book version. Afrykah WubSauda, I can't even begin to list your many talents. I am so grateful to have you as a friend and business partner. Thank you for all that you are. Thank you, Tracy Moore, for all of the hard work that you and Afrykah put in at Kreative Kollective and for being the first to read Strange Clouds in its entirety.

Last, but not least, an extra special thanks goes out to Ms. Bani Hines-Hudson for saying yes to writing the foreword and for being the first person to ever ask me to share my story. You have no idea what kind of monster you've created...lol.

Mad Love,

Che

TABLE OF CONTENTS

FOREWORD

As a reader of almost exclusively non-fiction, I questioned my ability to fully engage this work of fantasy from a person I have grown to highly respect without hint of the writer within. However, Cheketa would not allow me to defer to others. She insisted that I travel among "Strange Clouds" with her and for her. It was my good fortune to be stretched beyond my comfort zone.

'Strange Clouds' has revealed another talent expressed by one who has flown with her gifts under the radar. I already knew Cheketa as a brilliant businesswoman and survivor of a life filled with serious hard knocks along the way. Her personal story would have made a less persistent and confident person succumb to paralyzing depression. In 'Strange Clouds' she rises again! Through her characters, Cheketa, channels important lessons for an intergenerational wake-up call.

Thankfully, my lack of fantasy exposure was not a handicap in experiencing a multi-dimensional ride with Raysean and Keenan's family, friends, and foes. All throughout their adventures, mystical powers are harnessed to learn, to teach, and to defeat. The young people in this work reflect the innate wisdom, resourcefulness and determination that saved Cheketa and many others in spite of being cast as 'at-risk' and unsalvageable. Be ready. Within these pages, she speaks their/our language of the streets unapologetically.

Cheketa manages to integrate subjects that warrant more advocacies by the Black (and wider) community, including environmental injustice and respecting different intelligences.

9

She uses fantasy to provoke urgent conversations that forge instructive new paths. 'Strange Clouds' is deep and rich. The possibilities for this work to be used as an educational tool are many. I am honored to make the clarion call.

Bani Hines-Hudson
March 9, 2016

PREFACE

I'm so proud to say that Strange Clouds is my baby, but I haven't always felt that way. In the beginning, I was afraid to share my main characters, their real and sometimes abrasive dialogues, and complexities to the world. I was advised by conservative readers to tone down their dialect and swearing in effort to appeal to *everyone*, and believe me, I tried but my characters just did what any normal teenagers their ages would do – they shut me out.

I could feel their rebellion, refusing to allow me to channel them again until I grew "a pair". They each wanted so desperately to have permission for all of themselves to walk through that door. I felt inner reassurance of the importance of allowing my readers to experience each character in high definition. It was a crucial component in measuring the level of maturity that they were to exude. Literarily correct or poetic justice, I was uncertain of my delivery, so I found myself setting Strange Clouds down for many months after only writing the first few chapters.

Raysean began to speak again one evening as I sat on my deck staring at the night sky. Quite frankly he said, "Those ain't no muthafuckin' clouds."

I internally agreed. There wasn't a star in sight. My mind drifted off to recall nights so clear that stars appeared like millions of sparkling diamonds. I reluctantly glanced over at the never-ending smoke stack just behind my house in Rubbertown, and then rolled my eyes. I posed a reoccurring question to myself. What use was it to change our diets and exercise regimes when planes flew above our heads non-stop spraying fine heavy metals down on us, and while industrial companies located in residential areas, such as, Rubbertown were steadily releasing toxic chemicals into the air that we all breathe?

What was even more upsetting, was knowing that our own government has made it nearly impossible for these companies to ever be held accountable for the deaths that they have caused in their dishonest practices. I could feel Raysean putting the jumper cables on me, provoking me with his shared awareness. He challenged me, telling me that my "fuck cancer" statuses and articles that I frequently shared were not revolutionary enough, nor sufficient in the war to save our very lives.

He shot straight from the hip, with his proposition. He had punished me enough. The agreement was simple. He would allow me to watch, just as long as I recorded everything just as it occurred. No sugar coating. No cherries on top. I wouldn't censor them and they, in turn, would allow me to be a fly on the wall. Nevertheless, I still found myself searching for examples of my style of writing, needing validation to write a melanated fantasy story, uncensored and with unblinking honesty.

Strange Clouds Book One follows cousins, Raysean & Keenan, as they maneuver through and around life's obstacles with psychic and super powers. When they find themselves at the very center of a mysterious kidnapping, they soon discover that nothing and no one in the world are as they appear. It is a revolutionary backstory about how two "at risk" teens become leaders in a fight against secret societies and their vile and grotesque schemes to depopulate the world. This piece in particular translates the passion behind their relentless fight against villainous corporations and bigoted world super powers.

Strange Clouds was conceived from humility and born from witnessing and experiencing much pain and suffering. It's the kind of pain that comes from walking the medical green mile with many beloved family members and close friends that suffered, and ultimately, died from lupus and cancer over the recent years. Bedside vigils allowed for intimate insight into their transition processes. It was not only devastating, but also, provoking to watch the most vibrant and important people in my life become shriveled up shells of themselves. Terms like "make her/him more comfortable" began to sound more like code for slow euthanasia.

When April, a long-time friend of the family and mother of my daughter's sister died of cancer, the gloves came off and it was no holds barred. Cancer didn't seem to give 'two fucks' that she was only thirty-one years old and would leave behind five kids and it wouldn't give a damn about my daughter or me. April's doctor cited the environment to have been the cause of one of her cancers and I was reminded of the 'round the clock' smoke stacks that have polluted our neighborhood since we were kids. I could see so clearly the pattern, the money trail, and the culprits.

I found myself obsessed with investigating those responsible for taking the lives of those that I love so dearly. And, from under nearly every stone I turned were cancer-causing agents. After watching closely what I ate, I came to realize that, contrary to popular belief, high blood pressure didn't run in my family – bad habits did. Eating organically (non-GMO) and cooking "from scratch" became a way of life. But, by this time, my own daughter had developed lupus and I, myself, had taken notice to lumps growing beneath my arm and within my breast. I wasn't even old enough to have a mammogram.

The Universe was pushing the envelope. Cancer had just killed my grandmother and was drawing ever so nigh, still. I wasn't about that life – that cancer life, that chemo life, that radiation life, that breathing machine life, that pneumonia life, that bedsore life, or that septic infection life. I was overly aware that I didn't have the time that I thought I'd had. None of us do. All we have is now.

Strange Clouds is for everyone, but was especially written as a creative, entertaining, and informative tool with at-risk teens in mind. I felt that it was important for my protagonists, Raysean and Keenan, to be black in effort to curb the current propaganda driven perspectives instigated around the world by the media. It is my hope that it will bring awareness to racial, environmental, social, and religious injustices. With a focal on climate change, Strange Clouds also addresses; geoengineering also known as chemtrails, GMO's or Genetically Modified Organisms, metaphysics, and much more.

It is no coincidence that you are reading this book. My hopes are that the Strange Clouds series will not only inspire you, but provoke you to be the change that you want to see in the world.
Mad Love,
Che

CHAPTER ONE

HOMEROOM

Raysean's head nodded to the rhythm of the beat that Keenan snared out onto the desk in the classroom. The closer he got to homeroom, the more he began to feel it. The substitute teacher's high pitched "quiet pleases" and "settle downs" were perfectly timed adlibs to the sick freestyle that had nonchalantly entered his mind.

As he walked through the door, all eyes were on him. Keesha checked for his new J's. Hatin' Ass Jaquan peeked from the corner of his eyes. Red-boned Raeven smiled while whispering something into another girl's ear and Keenan gave a hard pause on the beat just before Raysean gestured in his direction. "Nah, my nigga, bring that beat back."

Raysean's hands bobbed and shoulders swayed as he surfed it like hang ten.

I'm up before the sunrise
First to hit the block
Lil bad muhfucka
With a pocket full of rocks
Soldier flip
And hit it quick
And lick the cash spot
Caution moving ready rock
Say you want it...stay on it
That hustling boy
It never stops....
I'm up before the sunrise

"Sir! Please have a seat."

Raysean eyeballed the rosy-cheeked sub with a, "Get the fuck out of my face," expression, but instead decided to give her a pass. He sensed that she wasn't challenging him, but was, instead, beyond frustrated. Raysean smirked, grabbed his crotch, and took the last available seat.

He promised his grandmother things wouldn't get out of hand like they had in the past. Raysean planned to make the best of this year, even if it meant pretending to be not as smart as his teachers. From as far back as he could remember he always had a knack for retaining information. He could see, hear, or read anything once and it would be forever embedded into his memory.

His grandmother first noticed his gift when she had forgotten her grocery list one Saturday afternoon. That day, four-year-old Raysean attentively watched his grandmother as he sat in the shopping cart. She fumbled through her purse in search of the menu for Pastor Crumlin's twenty-fifth anniversary.

The mini notebook with all of the ingredients and supplies written on it was officially M.I.A. Grandmaw quickly found herself agitated while trying to redraft the list from memory onto the backside of an envelope. Raysean detected her defeat and began playfully singing the list aloud. His grandmother was so amazed that she asked him to sing it again, but slowly, so that she could jot it all down.

Grandmaw recalled verifying the items on the list with Mrs. Crumlin over the phone the week prior, while scolding Raysean and his sister for playing in her living room. She wondered how he could recite the list verbatim after only hearing it once from another room during horseplay. Grandmaw shared her testimony of how God was "right on time" with the church congregation the morning of the anniversary. Women wearing oversized hats jumped up and down and shouted, "Hallelujah!" The church attributed the miracle of memory to be a blessing delivered to God's highly favored.

From then on, Raysean was Grandmaw's human telephone book, lottery number generator, and personal calendar.

Ms. Rosy-cheeks sat down, rolled her eyes, and began roll call.

"Rachel Adler."

"Here."

"Steven Bruce."

"Here."

"Ashley Dumfarht."

"Here."

Hatin Ass Jaquan made a fart noise with his mouth and the crowded room erupted in laughter. Raysean eyeballed Jaquan as a reminder of the promise that he made to him last year when he made fun of the heavyset timid girl that sat in front of them. Raysean fumed to himself.

He been doing that stupid shit since the sixth grade. We in the ninth grade and he still petty. How you gon' pick on somebody that don't fight back? I already checked for his mark ass though. He can't fight and his heart pump Kool-Aid. He know it and he know I know it, too. I can see it in his eyes, the way that they run from mines when I catch his peeking ass. Pussy nigga. I can see it in his body language, the way that he tries to swell up when I walk by him. I'll mop him. I can't wait for the day when that nigga forget who he talking to and I have to stomp a mudhole in him.

Raysean had a reputation for being a badass and even a bully at times. He didn't see himself that way, though. He had a strong sense of justice, often dubbing himself as a bully's bully. He was average in stature, yet in moments of rage could be capable of extraordinary strength and skill.

Raysean was currently under probation supervision, because he broke his mother's boyfriend's arm during one of their many drunken disputes. Her boyfriend, Montez, was "over" the family visit and was ready to leave. It didn't matter to him that he was the father of Raysean's little sisters. He had business to take care of.

A heated argument ensued and Grandmaw put Raysean's mother, Nadine - and her boyfriend, Montez out of her house.

Standing on her porch with her hands on her hips, Grandmaw reinforced her actions, "Ya'll get away from here with all that damn drama! I don't want all that mess around me or these kids! If you want to see yo babies, you betta act like you got some damn sense. Cause' I ain't wit' all that. You betta ask some body!"

When Montez threatened to take his daughters with them, Raysean stomped out into the yard and violently snatched the wrist attached to the hand that was threatening to put him "in a child's place". Raysean simultaneously leaped up into the air, wrapped his legs around Montez's arm and flipped him onto his back atop of the moist grass. Arching his back, Raysean hyperextended Montez's arm while pinning his legs across his chest. The iron flavor from nearly biting through his own lip and the slight give were the only things that brought Raysean back to reality.

The police were called and the officer that transported him to the Jefferson County Youth Correctional Facility observed a justified expression on Raysean's face as he inspected him through the rear-view mirror of the squad car.

He thought to himself.

I hope this punk doesn't slip through the cracks.

One glance at Montez's arm convinced the officer that a professional had broken it. The officer had been the lead MMA instructor at "The G.O.A.T MMA Gym" for the past seven years. He had seen his fair share of injuries while employed there and Montez's dislocated elbow was the worst arm bar injury that he had ever seen. He had no choice except to charge Raysean with Assault with a deadly instrument.

The deadly instrument – his body.

Assault I was amended down, because it turned out that Raysean had never taken martial arts, as the officer suspected. He learned the arm bar technique after observing it, just once, when it was flawlessly executed during a *UFC* title match.

22

Bbbbbbzzzzzddddzzzzzz. Raysean ran his fingers along his back pocket to feel for his smart phone and then pulled it out. It was buzzing, but the caller's name wasn't displayed. It was Keenan's version of the *made you look game*, with an electronic twist. Keenan got a kick out of setting off Raysean's cellphone and then yelling into his head. Telepathy was never something that Raysean could ever get used to. He preferred verbal conversations to cerebral shouts any day.

Keenan was excited about the newest trick added to his repertoire. He had been doing it to Raysean all summer - showing off his newest ability, telekinesis. Keenan discovered that he could move objects with his mind on the basketball court in an intense game of *twenty-one* during summer break. The score was 20-20 and it was Keenan's ball.

Basketball was the one thing that Keenan felt better at than Raysean and he charged down the cracked pavement with sheer determination to keep it that way.

Raysean reached in, stripped the ball from him, and laid it up against the backboard. It bounced and wobbled around the rim as the boys bumped and spun out preparing for the rebound. The ball teetered too far in the wrong direction and Raysean let out a loud scream as he jumped up and slapped the side of it. The net whipped back and forth like Willow Smith's hair.

"Game!"

"Yea, but look at all these scratches and shit all over me! You don' stretched my shirt all out, dawg! You weak!" Keenan huffed.

"Come on, mane! I got scratches all over me *toooo!*"

Holding the ball above his head, Raysean displayed his battle wounds. Keenan sulked and imagined snatching the ball from his cousin's grip. The ball instantly ripped through his fingers and shot in his direction like a pass from *Lebron*, nearly knocking Keenan to the ground when he caught it. Grinning and saucer-eyed, they looked at each other. They were thinking the same thing.

The NBA!!!!!

Raysean spent the rest of that sweltering day watching Keenan hit *all net* from every angle of the court as their hoop dreams set in the golden horizon.

Ms. Rosy-cheeks called the next name.

"Keenan Hughes."

"Here."

"Jaquan Jackson."

"Here."

"Raysean Lewis."

"Here."

"Eeehhh!"

Keenan launched a mental scream directly into his cousin's head. "That was so fuckin sick!!!!" he said regarding their chemistry of rhythm and rhyming. Raysean flinched and turned his head towards the floor. His hands fought the urge to cradle his ears, knowing that his reaction would appear weird to his classmates. However, Ms. Rosy-cheeks was much more obvious. The mug that she had been holding came crashing to the floor spilling a steamy vanilla-crème concoction all over it. The bell rang and students simultaneously burst into chatter while piling into the hallways from every classroom.

Keenan and Raysean were just about the last students to tip toe past Ms. Rosy-cheeks and her awkward hot mess, when she said, "Mr. Hughes and Mr. Lewis, I need to speak with you before you leave."

Raysean stuttered his steps, but got an instant nudge in the back from Keenan to keep it moving.

"What, no encore?" Ms. Rosy-cheeks asked cockily without moving her lips. Keenan's nudge was now a shove through a sea of students entering the room for their first period class with her. The boys swiftly swam against the current of haters and congratulators.

"Stop pushing me, man!"

Keenan was so close to Raysean that they looked like conjoined twins. He was in full fight or flight mode, because up until that morning, Raysean was the only person that he shared the gift of telepathy with. But now Ms. Rosy-cheeks. Something about her—dark and deceptive, bold and determined, powerful and familiar.

"If you step on the back of my new shoes, dawg!" Raysean warned his cousin.

"Why are you acting like you didn't hear her! You kill me, dawg, always tryna' front like you hard...like don't nothing get to you!" Keenan fumed.

"So, I'm frontin' cuz' I don't freak out and get all scared of stuff like you do?"

Raysean made no apologies for his endless reserve of fearlessness. His gift of empathy promoted it. Knowing how a person felt unmasked them, leaving him only with the omniscience of their emotions in their purest form.

He could tell within seconds of meeting a person whether or not they were a threat to him. His conclusions were the results of lightening fast predictabilities equated from probability, possibility, and empathy.

Raysean found it difficult to exert his sentiments into words without being offensive to Keenan, so he beamed it to him, instead. His auric essence extended out and merged with Keenan's, allowing a potentially complicated conversation - to be energetically transferred in the most harmonious way. He then felt his cousin's energy instantly calm and settle.

CHAPTER TWO

LOTUS

Lotus took another glance at her class schedule and felt even more overwhelmed. *This sucks!* The immensely loud school bell clanging in her ears sounded like she had just won a jackpot and her prize was an avalanche of ninth-graders snowballing in her direction. Her Auntie Qi was right. Public school was *so* overrated.

The doors to every room in the long shiny hallway popped open at once just like they do at the Kentucky Derby and students spilled into the elongated space trying to *Win Place* or *Show*.

"Don't forget to breathe and always protect yourself," Auntie Qi's voice echoed in her memory box.

Lotus closed her eyes and began to surround herself in pure white light to prevent the high-speed clickety clacks and squeaks and sqacks of borrowed stilettos and expensive sneakers from executing a well-planned play against her. She was sensitive to the energies of others. She could not only feel their joy and pain, but could also sense their negative intentions; as well as, their highest good. Lotus had to make the best of her circumstances. She was afraid, but Auntie Qi reassured her that this was the hard and necessary part of the vision.

Auntie Qi was never wrong.

Lotus took in a deep breath and opened her eyes to find herself inside of the most beautiful transparent bubble. Its radius was about three feet all around her and reflected the most vivid swirly hues from the kaleidoscope of colors students wore for the first day of school fashion show.

Lotus glanced around at the students zipping past her. She was in search of someone like herself. Lotus knew that there were over one hundred thousand gifted children spread throughout the United States and there were more than double that in China.

27

She knew, not only because she was told about their existence; but also because she could feel them. She could feel them like her very own skin.

The locker next to her opened with a loud clang. She turned her head to the side, so that she could get a really good *discrete* look at its occupant. Lotus could not only see with her eyes, but also with her ears, nose, mouth, tongue, armpits, hands and feet. She pretended to unlock the combination to her locker. Staring at the numbers on the padlock, Lotus visualized them shifting, morphing and zooming. Her perception of the hustle and bustle in the hallway suddenly froze. The teenage freeway silenced. There was no movement. No cellphone chatter. No more selfie's. No more laughter and the fly on the wall's wings went from two hundred flaps a second to an eye's blink. The only sound she heard was from the beat of her own heart.

She thought to herself.

Now, that's better.

Lotus slowly lifted her head, with her eyes being the last to rise. Her toffee colored eyes were, now, glowing the most beautiful crystal blue. They had the likeness of an untouched blue lagoon, no ending, clean and clear. She did not have to look around, because she had better than perfect direct and peripheral vision. She saw everyone and everything in that space, and not just what they looked like. She saw into their very souls.

 "Whoa...wait...who are they?" Lotus thought to herself as she watched two guys...cousins...hurrying through the crowd. They were protected, but barely. They had more holes in their aura than Swiss cheese, but still protected. Lotus recalled the aura teachings that she received under Auntie Qi's tutelage. She got the impression that the boy in front had issues with anger, despite being of a deep compassionate nature. The one behind him suffered from a severe lack of confidence and was of an unconditionally forgiving nature. She realized that they were running from someone when she locked eyes with the boy leading the way.

She thought to herself.

Did he just see me? I mean, of course, he saw me...but did he see see me? If he didn't, I know for a fact that she did.

Lotus was being glared at by Ms. Rosy Cheeks and it weirded her out. And, although she doesn't normally stare for fear of an unwanted invitation, she broke her own three-second rule and still got nothing. The teacher was shielding herself. She was certain of it. Lotus was one of very few that could break shields, but there was no need to at the moment. She was there for a reason known only to Auntie Qi and she would follow her instructions to the letter. Auntie Qi was a master kuten, a Tibetan oracle renowned for her precise accuracy and predictability. She was like a walking crystal ball.

Lotus, awkwardly, did an about-face and blended with the flow of traffic.

CHAPTER THREE

LUNCH

"Aye, dawg, get a chocolate milk", Keenan asked Raysean for like the upteempth time. Raysean gave him a side-eyed gas face. "Fuck on' wid all et' bullshit," vomited from his lips. Raysean thought.

I don't spare no muhfucka that be trying to play me – playing or not. See, muhfucka's be trying to, light weight, see how far they can go witchu...be laughing shit off and be serious and shit.

"Damn, Raysean...cuz, et's fa us, dawg?"

He looked his cousin in the eyes, shook his head and said, "Cuz, I done told you that I don't drink et' slimy ass shit. Who tha fuck won' drink some shit that you gotta chase wit water afterwards? Et' shit be cramping my stomach up and shit, dawg. Fuck et' nasty ass shit."

"Nigga, you trippin', chocolate milk is *THUNDA!* Plus, it fill you up when a nigga stomach be touching his back, dawg. You ain't gotta drink it. Get it for me."

Keenan's voice was raspy and he spoke with a certified Louisville drawl.

Instead, of "there" he said "ver", preferred "hhrrr" over "here" and he used "thunda" for every word that he couldn't find an appropriate word to describe the highest degree of which he enjoyed something.

"Nah, nigga, kill *yaself.*"

"Name one person that died from drinking some chocolate milk, dawg!"

"Actually, it is poisonous," said a soft feminine mixed accent injecting itself into their debate.

Raysean's head turned towards the poetic voice. First sight of her made him wet. His underarms perspired. His forehead moistened. His hands were clammy. His mouth salivated. Raysean fought his body's urges to bulge, provoking a thousand

31

butterflies to take flight in his stomach. Her slanted exotic eyes were like tiger-eye gems, set perfectly, above her bronze high cheekbones - *a sign of Indian in the family for sure* – he thought. She had plush pink pouty lips and the black wavy silk, on top of her head, was wound up into a perfectly messy bun. Her lips began to move. He can't tell you what she said. Raysean couldn't hear her. He just knew that they danced like they were competing on the hit show *Dancing with the Stars*. Her candy colored orifice kissed every syllable and clung together like honey between fingertips. They opened and closed to a soft pooch. He'd bet anything that they tasted just like *Watermelon Now or Laters*. They stopped. He was still staring.

"Posa –what, bruh?" Keenan asked her attempting to save his cousin from the awkward moment.

"Bruh?" she asked.

"Where you from? We call err 'body et'. Don't trip, lil mama," was Keenan's quick recovery.

"Po-sil-ac. P.O.S.I.L.A.C also known as the chemical rBGH. It's found in over ninety percent of America's milk, yet it's banned in over twenty-seven countries. It causes breast and gastro-intestinal cancer," Lotus replied.

"We all gotta die of something and when I go, I wanna go in a *poooooooool* of chocolate milk", Keenan jokingly shot back. Raysean noticed her sliding an empty tray along the metal rails. He glanced down at the tray, into her eyes and then back down at the tray.

"So, whatchu gon' do? Die of starvation *and* dehydration?" He asked sarcastically.

"I'm clearly not starving."

The way that she said that, "I'm clearly not starving," he assumed that she was giving him permission to check her out. Boldly, he eyeballed her up and down. Down and up. Forward and back. Back and forward. She tilted her head to the side and raised her left brow. Raysean shot her a smirk of approval and digressed.

"Whatchu mixed with?"

He considered her too dark to be Asian and too curvy to be anything else but black.

She turned her nose up at his tray and said, "Certainly not, GMO's."

"Th'fucks et'?

"You kiss your mom with that mouth?"

"I don't have a *mom*. I have a *mama* and hell muhfuck'n naw we don't kiss," he said giving her the *stupid face* along with a laugh. It sounded like a mix between the evil wizard from *The Smurfs* cartoon "Gargamel" and a hyena's laugh. The sound of plastic sliding against metal suddenly stopped.

He cursed himself in his head.

Damn. I'm about to lose my girl before I make her my girl. Usually when I fuck up, I stand my ground. Might as well. Fuck it. A muhfucka don't spare me none. But, this girl...she makes me want to hold my head down and turn my eyes away before she does. A chick like her'll make me change my status to "in a relationship" and only lames do et' weak shit. She's thuuunda, though and ain't no bitch in this school touch'n her.

Fiending for her to break her silence, Raysean asked," What's GNO."

"GMO. It stands for Genetically Modified Organism and it's not what it is. It's what it isn't."

"What it ain't?"

"Food."

"8583", Keenan recited, giving the lunch lady his free & reduced meal identification number.

He picked up his tray, did a little happy dance, and made a hard left - being the first to exit the chow line.

"8642", Raysean said in a low tone.

"What?"

"8 6 4 2", he repeated distorting his voice while imitating sign language.

Lotus noticed a red puff of a smoky-like substance leaking from his aura. "You should really watch that."

"Watch what", Raysean asked picking up his tray while trying to re-locate his cousin. "Your temperament," was Lotus' gentle reply.

"She knows that she heard me the first time," he defensively shot back while giving his cousin a head nod in confirmation of his whereabouts.

Keenan was sitting with a group of about ten "turnt up" teens. Some were seemingly dancing to theme songs heard only on the inside of their own heads; while others were giving each other hugs, dap, high-fives and really cool handshakes. They all motioned for him to sit with them and announced his name in unison as if they were his personal cheerleading squad. "Riiiiiiiizzzzzy!"

Before joining his followers, he took a few steps and added, "Plus, I hate repeating myself."

He anticipated her silky mellifluous accent behind him, but a canyon of nothingness echoed in its place. Raysean glanced over his shoulder to see her walking away in the opposite direction heading towards a table of none. She wore an altered off-the-shoulder kimono styled blouse that was fitted around the waist, some fly yoga leggings and a pair of earthy thong sandals.

Her hips sashayed side to side, rocking against her Tibetan hemp knapsack, like the bow on a prodigy's violin. Her derriere bounced to the rhythm of the nervous thuds in Raysean's chest. She walked away and flashed him an innocent smile after a perfectly timed over-the-shoulder glance.

She sat down at the nearest empty table and removed her lunch from her sack. The first was a container of momos, delicious spicy Tibetan dumplings from scratch, an Auntie Qi specialty. There was a smaller container of sweet and spicy red dipping sauce, some lemons, and a bottle of Fiji water. Never once looking up, she began to smile and count down to herself, "Five, Four, Three, Two..."

"You going to just stand there?"

She looked up at a curious Raysean standing before her. He pulled out a chair from the table and sat down.

"What's up?"

"Nothing", she said sliding a peeled lemon down the spout of her spring water.

"You making lemonade?"

"No, I'm alkalizing my water."

"Awe," Raysean pretended to understand. Knowing that he didn't, she began to explain.

"An alkaline body is a cancer-free body..."

Cutting her off, Raysean asked, "You never answered my question."

"I'm Tibetan and black."

"You're black then, because anything mixed with black is black."

"Is that so?"

"That's what white people think, even though, you lookin' like *Tiger Woods* luh susta and shit," he teased her.

"What's your...?" he attempted to ask her name.

"Lotus Butsugen," she interrupted, folding her hands together like she was going to pray and then raising them up to her forehead in a slight bowing motion.

"Lotus Boo," he said flirting with her and repeating the same hand motion back to her with a cheesy grin. He officially felt like a cornball.

"What...?" he attempted to deflect by asking her what bus she rode.

"I don't ride a bus. My aunt drives me to school."

"My name is Ray..."

"I know. Raysean Lewis."

"How you know my name?

"I read it off of your school id," Lotus said toying with him.

He felt for his id and confirmed that it was still hooked to his belt loop and tucked inside of his pant's pocket. His forehead crinkled as he experienced temporary lethologica.

The bell rang and an airy high-pitched voice called out into the intercom," Raysean Lewis, Keenan Hughes, and Lotus Butsugen, please come to the main office immediately. Raysean Lewis, Keenan Hughes, and Lotus Butsugen, please come to the main office immediately."

Raysean looked in Keenan's direction with a puzzled look on his face.

"Aye, dawg!" Keenan screeched into his head.

It annoyed Raysean when he did that, because it was usually unexpected and often came through loud like front row at a rock concert. Raysean not only hears it in his head, but feels exactly how his cousin feels at the moment the message is being transmitted, except magnified. If he is mad enough, it will come through like a gavel of lightning coursing through him.

Butterflies in Keenan's stomach felt like a *flight of the conchords* to Raysean. To Raysean, Keenan's emotions often felt like how he would imagine it would feel like to walk through a rain cloud - heavy and turbulent.

Lotus waved her hands before Raysean's eyes to regain his attention.

"Are you okay?" She asked noticing a change in his breathing, as well as a, disconnect from her.

She turned and looked into Keenan's direction. The cousin's eyes were fixated on each other. She noticed that they were connected by a very thin cord of light that was straight in some places, spiraled in others and stretched across the lunchroom. It reminded her of an old telephone cord, except it appeared to have life. It waved subtly like the strand of a mother's hair against her sleeping baby's breath. They were having a full-blown conversation.

"Why you keep doing that shit, bruh?"

"That was her!"

"Who?!! Nigga, you fuckin' my shit up!"

"The bitch from homeroom!"

"You tripping, dawg!"

"Naw, bruh, I ain't trippin'. I told you that she *jumped* in my head."

"Look, man...whatchu tryna do?" Raysean preferred it *straight from the hip.*

"Let's leave, bruh."

The suggestion would normally have been Raysean's, but he was on probation.

"Quit being dramatic, dawg. It might not be nothing. If it is, *then,* we'll leave, aight?"

"Cool," Cuzzo replied reluctantly.

CHAPTER FOUR

MAIN OFFICE

Raysean's fingers tips pressed hard against the heavy frosted glass door of the main office, as he held it open for Keenan to catch it.

"Nigga, come on! Ain't nobody bout' ta hold the door open for you all day."

He thought to himself.

This nigga scared to death of the bitch from homeroom. Tryna walk all slow and shit. Come the fuck on, nigga!

"Damn, nigga, fa real doe?" Keenan asked after hearing Raysean's thoughts.

He then said, "Finish him," and playfully gave Raysean a light one-two to the side just before he walked under his arm instead of catching the door.

"You act like a nigga can't hear you, bitch," Keenan laughed. Raysean let go of the door in hopes of him being hit with it just in time. It missed, so he tried clipping his feet instead. Raysean clipped his back foot and then Keenan started doing one of his silly happy dances. It began with a one-legged hop and ended with the *Nay Nay*.

"Go head on' Chris Brown ass nigga," Raysean said and the kids sitting in office burst out in tears.

Keenan leaned back slightly, stuck out his tongue and flashed him his infamous middle fingers.

"Can I help you?" The counselor, Mrs. Cole, asked him.

"Yaaaaaaah" Keenan said coolly. The audience laughed again.

"Let me tell you something, Mr. Hughes. I told your butt last year that it ain't gon' be non' of that this year. This year is up to you, luh boy. Now, I'm going to ask you one more time. Don't make me hurt you."

Keenan started cheesing hard. He's been in love with Mrs. Cole since the sixth grade. Every time she was around, he would always cock his head sideways and say to his cousin, "Damn, she got a *Nicki* ass."

And with his head cocked the same way, "Damn, she do," was Raysean's usual response.

"I'm sorry, Mama," Keenan mocked.

For some reason, most of the "problem" students called her that. It was probably, because she was always acting like somebody's mama.

"Uuuhnnn huuuuh...be good, luh boy. What do you need?"

"Uuhnnn know, ya'll called me down hhrrr."

"Sign in and have a seat."

Her eyes shot in Raysean's direction. One of her eyebrows was slightly raised into a perfect arch. She reminded him of "Saaaaaandra" from *227*, except her hair was more like Halle Berry's. Her lips were tooted to the side like she "wish the hell they would" act a fool on the first day of school.

"We gon' have us a good year, Mr. Lewis?"

"We had us a good year last year, Mrs. Cole."

"Uuuhnnn huuuuh," she dragged out.

"Whatchu you need, Raysean", she asked him irritated by his mere presence.

"Somebody just called us down to the office."

"Who called you down here?" she asked crossing her arms like she was about to blink him away.

"I don't know. The intercom lady, I guess," He replied snorting out his words.

"Aight, ya'll not gon' start this year off acting a fool. Try me if you want to."

Raysean looked around at the white people in the office like, "Ya'll gon' just let her talk to me like this." Some had the "get him" look on their faces and the others turned deaf ears and blind eyes.

"I love you too, Mrs. Cole," Raysean said calling a truce.

"Sign in and sit down, luh boy. Let me see what's going on," she said.

Raysean signed "$ Rizzy $" and turned to look for a seat. The first seat was taken by two girls lapped up, talking about what they were going do to some "bitch" if she tried to lie about some "dumb shit". Mrs. Cole said something slick to them about their mouths being "too slick". In the second chair, was Keenan trying to make advances at the two girls in the first chair. He started singing, "wifey, girlfriend, and mistress."

They all started laughing.

Keenan didn't care. He was girl crazy. He could be found in the middle of a group of girls at any party. They loved sticking their fingers deep inside of his dimples and twisting them. He was a lady's man, always appearing to just know the right words to say to them. Really. He listened to their thoughts and currently held the title for getting the most phone numbers at the end of a day, because he only flirted with girls that he knew already liked him.

Sitting cross-legged in the chair next to Keenan was Lotus. Her eyes were locked on Raysean. She had the most inquisitive look on her face. She glanced away when he took the wall beside of her. Her energy felt ticklely to him. He made her nervous or was it him that was nervous? Raysean closed his eyes and sensed her heart rate increasing. His mouth was dry. She took a sip of her lemon water. His mouth clenched and slavered from its tartness.

"How come you don't put sugar in that stuff," he asked her.

"Lotus Bus-," Ms. Rosy Cheeks interrupted in a half attempt at Lotus' last name.

"Butsugen," Lotus said back to her.

The educator motioned for her to come into the office. Lotus smiled at Raysean just as she walked through the door. She smelled sweet to him, like homemade vanilla ice cream.

"Lotus. That's a pretty name for a very pretty girl," the woman said as she closed the door behind them. Lotus shyly nodded her head acknowledging Ms. Rosy-cheek's compliment.

"Please have a seat."

Lotus sat down in a heavy burgundy colored leather chair with copper studs running down its back and sides. It was the perfect chair to curl up and read a good book.

She began to look around the room. Accolades filled nearly every inch of the walls. The name "Eric Wright, Principal" was engraved on a crystal name plaque and its placement was flush with the cherry oak desk. Lotus then snuck a quick peek at the woman's nametag. The woman removed her jacket before Lotus could get a good look. She softly draped it over the back of the chair that she sat in. With her hands hidden under the desk, she clasped them together on her lap. Her face was tranquil and confident. There was an awkward silence before she spoke.

"I called you down here, because we do not have any immunizations records on file for you," she said breaking the deafening quietness.

Lotus instantly felt deception.

"Immunization?" Lotus repeated back to her in the form of a question.

She was no novice at this. Auntie Qi trained her to avoid leading questions from all authorities. She considered herself a pro at naivety, although she was far from it.

"Yes, immunization. When was the last time that you had shots, sweetheart?"

"Shots?" Lotus said avoiding the question while making a shooting gesture with her fingers.

"No," the woman playfully mocked her accent as she reached into a drawer of the desk and laid a loaded syringe on top of it. An alarmed Lotus quickly offered to call Auntie Qi to sort it all out. This was an Auntie Qi protocol.

"Sure, please call your Aunt," she replied as if she had all the time in the world. Lotus pulled out her cell phone, scrolled through her call log, and tapped "Anay".

It means auntie in her first tongue.

No signal.

Lotus hang up on her end and promised to pass the message.

"I wish that it was that simple, but, fortunately, JCPS does not allow unvaccinated students to attend school with vaccinated students. We can vaccinate you here or will have to send you home until the proper vaccination documents are in your file," she said opening up a manila folder.

"I'm afraid that we will have to suspend you until we receive an updated immunization certificate for you."

"Ok, when?"

"Immediately."

"I need to try my auntie again. She picks me up."

"Try calling her again. Either way, I'll more than likely, be giving you a ride."

The offer was a red flag. They found her.

She remembered Auntie Qi's constant assurances.

You have to let them take you...relax and trust the process.

On the brink of a panic, she tried calling her auntie again. Auntie Qi picked up on the second ring. As protocol, they began to speak in their native language. Lotus got up and walked towards the window. The dialect was loud and pronounced, fast and thick. It had grungy undertones at some points and smooth and sultry overtones in others. They were having a very emotional exchange that appeared to end abruptly.

Lotus turned wearing a very grim look. She placed her phone into her knapsack and a rehearsed smile on her face. She was immediately startled. Sitting in the chair, behind the heavy desk, was an ebony woman finishing up a text message. Lotus couldn't believe that she was standing before, Saada, one of the most powerful shape shifters in the world. She not only had the power to take on the appearance of those that she has killed; but she also had the ability to absorb their powers, and gifts. Saada laid the cell phone on the desk and slowly looked up.

Lotus felt a pang in her stomach that knocked the wind out of her. She instinctively bolted for the door. It locked on its own before her very eyes. She grabbed the knob and attempted her escape. She mustered up two violent shakes before she tensed up into a full body muscle spasm. She tried to let out a scream, but the ligaments in her neck tightened like a noose. She felt a firm touch in the small of her back and in her mind she heard, "Now now, Lotus. This won't hurt a bit."

Auntie Qi, Raysean and Keenan's heads shot up into attention. They all heard the blood curdling psychic scream, although, they were in separate locations. Auntie Qi quickly made a dash towards the front door. She grabbed her keys from an armoire in the foyer and slid her bare feet into the sandals that lay beneath it. As she swung open the front door, she ran into an asian man wearing an expensive tailored suit and dark sunglasses standing on her front porch. He embraced her in a tight hug, while injecting something into her neck that made her body go limp. With her eyes wide open, he carried her back into the house.

Meanwhile, Keenan and Raysean anxiously discerned each other. While still leaning against the wall, Raysean discretely wiggled the doorknob behind him. He saw that it was locked.

"Aye, dawg, call her," Raysean said eagerly to his cousin.

"What's her number?"

"Quit acting stupid, dawg, and jump in her head!"

"Nah, dawg, just knock on the door."

"And say what, dawg?! Call her, mane, sump'in ain't right."

"Yea, and make me look like the fuck'n weirdo, right?"

"BRUH!!!!!!"

Raysean was completely panicked, so Keenan reluctantly closed his eyes and tried to imagine Lotus' face. He saw himself sitting on a bench courtside at Russell Lee Park. This was his "safe place," the place where he felt the most in control. His foster mother taught him to think of a safe place whenever he had those dreams of flying. She referred to it as Astral Projection. She told him that it happened to people who have the ability "to walk between worlds." She sometimes even took him with her to drumming classes where he described people that awoke from trances to tell stories of animals giving them "powerful messages."

His foster mother meant well, but all that stuff scared the crap out of him, especially the night that he awoke to see an older man sitting by her bed. He saw the man stroke her hair ever so softly over and over. The next morning, she was sitting at the table crying. When he asked her why she was crying, she told him that her grandfather had just passed away. A few days later, they attended the funeral of her grandfather and he was freaked out to see the same older man standing alongside of the casket that his body was lying in.

That night Keenan attracted spirits like a moth to a flame. It was the same night that, after awakening to his scream, Keenan's foster mother taught him to go to his "safe place." For a while, he preferred his safe place over the real world. Especially, when his counselor at the Seven Counties' Mental Health Facility decided that it was best for him to be seen by a specialist. When he stopped speaking, the specialist diagnosed him with Autism. The Post Traumatic Stress Disorder, and Paranoid Schizophrenia diagnosis' were a given, and were attributed to his night frights and ghosts that he reported seeing and hearing. His foster mother didn't agree with his diagnosis and being under the government's thumb certainly didn't help matters.

Keenan often complained that the medicine they prescribed him made him slow and worsened his dreams and visions. It exposed him, making him vulnerable and defenseless. Visualizing himself surrounded in white light, served to be no longer effective while Keenan was taking the psychiatric drugs. This opened the door for him to be tortured by malevolent entities without end.

When Keenan joined Raysean a year later to live at their grandmother's house, his cousin realized that he "acted different". Raysean cracked jokes on him constantly about it, calling him a zombie. The more that Keenan retreated inside of himself, the more "jumping" in his head became easier and "jumping" out much more hard. Keenan felt like his mind was being overtaken by the random voices that were crashing there. One day, while bouncing a basketball, Raysean said, "If I were you, I'd fake like I was taking that medicine, but I wouldn't really take it for real."

A loud voice rudely interjected saying, "Fuck him!"

Keenan covered his ears and bowed his head in tears. The voice kept repeating it over and over again like a scratched record. Raysean grabbed his cousin's hands from the sides of his face and said, "Nigga, fuck's wrong wit chu? This shit chu' on got you crazy ass a muhfucka. You gon' be like Old Man Grady and shit!" Raysean's words came across as a sarcastic whisper in comparison to the crazy megaphone man in his head. Keenan replied blank-faced and wild-eyed. His face no longer looked familiar to Raysean.

"Bruh, what's wrong?"

"A voice just told me to kill you."

"What???!!!"

"He just told me to kill you."

"Ahhhh, forreal, my nigga?"

Keenan's energy felt disgusting to Raysean.

"And what chu' gon' do? Kill me?"

That terrified him. Keenan could never fathom taking the life of anyone, let alone his cousin who was more like a brother. Yet, he also couldn't think of living the rest of his life that way, either. He hated to admit it, but he'd thought about it - silencing the voice by doing what it said.

One day, he just went off the psychotic drugs cold turkey. It was pretty easy. Raysean suggested that they sell his pills, refills and all. That summer they were some "caked up" nine-year-olds. It was the summer that he stopped hearing the voices of spirit and started to hear the thoughts of everyone else, with the exception of Lotus. Keenan could not hear or pick up anything from her. She wasn't like everyone else. It was like she had a protective field around her.

He could see her face, but barely. There was so much light surrounding her that he felt as though he was nearly blinded. Keenan placed his astral hand above his brow to create a visor effect. He tried walking up to her, but he couldn't penetrate the light. It was a barrier of some sort. He could only get so close, before he would bounce back like there were two giant invisible balls between them. As Keenan squinted to see more clearly, he noticed a woman with her. She was darker than mahogany. The woman sharply peered in his direction.

Keenan's eyes popped open. He had the look of panick written all over his face. Raysean searched his demeanor for something, anything positive. Nothing. Driven by his intuition, Raysean unclipped his I.D. badge from his waistline and slid its edge into the crack where the door met the wall. He heard a click and felt the door give. He pretended to accidentally stumble backwards and spilled into the room with his back to them.

"Whoa...sorr-," his words escaped his thoughts after seeing what he saw.

A breeze from the precipice of a brisk autumn storm sent the blinds flapping turbulently into the wind. Sheets of paper funneled around the room. A manila folder levitated wildly from

47

the desk and fell at his feet. In the middle of the cover was a big red stamp that read "TOP SECRET" and in the top right hand corner was the name "TENZIN". A picture of Lotus as a child peered from inside of it. Raysean quickly scooped up the folder and its contents, stuffed them in his pants, pulled his shirt over them and then belted out a bombastic scream for Mrs. Cole.

He ran to the window to catch a glimpse of her kidnappers. There was no *them*. Just *her*. A woman with a complexion extracted from cocoa beans and skin smoother than polished opal was dressed exactly like the teacher from homeroom. She pushed Lotus' sack covered head into the backseat of the all black vehicle that awaited them, looked Raysean in the eyes, shot him a wink and jumped in.

The all black everything, four door Chevy Camaro, nearly plowed into Terry Road's rush hour traffic. The license plate read "CNTCME".

As it sped off, he heard a frightened Lotus yelp into his mind. Her voice was heavy and stuck with him like a snowfall to wet pavement.

She screamed, "Raysean, Heeeeelp!

CHAPTER FIVE

FOUR DOOR CAMARO

"Let me get this right. You said that it was a black *four* door Chevy Camaro?" Detective Nunnely sounded like he was auditioning for the *Dukes of Hazard*.

"Yehhhh…an all black *err'thang fo' do'* Chevy Camaro," Raysean responded.

"What's makes you think that it was an all black err'thang fo' do' Camaro," he mocked Raysean.

"Cuz I know Camaro lights."

"You a collector or something?"

Raysean side-eyed the officer. *This muhfucka's a clown,* he thought.

"Nah, man, I know Camaro lights, bruh."

"Tell me more about the woman that allegedly took her."

"Allegedly?"

"What can you tell me about her kidnapper?

"Aye, pump yo breaks, man. What chu' mean by allegedly, bruh? You tryna say a nigga lying or sump'n?"

"Was she black? White? Young? Old?"

"She was black," Raysean cynically responded.

"Young? Old?"

"Old like you."

"So, she looked to be in her late thirties, you're saying?"

"Yeh."

"Mr. Lewis, would you mind explaining why you're on probation?" The detective asked throwing in a curveball.

"Yeh."

"Yes, what?"

"I mind."

"Do you have a guilty conscience?"

"Guilty conscience for what, mane? I got two weeks left and I'm good. I did err'thang I was s'posed to do, dawg."

"I ain't yo "dawwwwg", brother."

"I ain't cho' brother, dawg," Raysean snarled.

Raysean leaned back in his chair and crossed his arms. Grandmaw perked up in her chair.

"Ray-Ray, what I tell you, boy, bout' cho mowlf? I don' told'ja *now* that yo mowlf gon' get cho' butt in some serious trouble one day," she warned him like he was a defiant slave running away from "massa".

"But, Grandmaw, you act like you ain't just hear him being prejudiced towards me. "

"Prejudiced?" Detective Nunnely interjected.

Prejudiced was the last thing that the detective considered himself to be. His best friend was black and he even voted for Obama.

"Please excuse my grandson. He's going through a really tough time. His mama in the streets. His daddy locked up. I'm taking care of him and his sisters til' my son come home. I also got my daughter's children and she's deceased. I'm doing the best I can wit' what I got. He's a good kid...just had a rough time...ets all," Grandmaw said with watery eyes.

"Son, that attitude of yours is gonna get you in a lot trouble one day. You're going to find yourself in jail, if you don't straighten yourself out. You got your grandmother over here in tears..." Detective Nunnely said just before being interrupted by Raysean.

"Aight, mane," he interjected with a slow head nod and a gesture of surrender.

Raysean hated when someone upset his Grandmaw. It made him violent. In the past, it's even gotten him into physical altercations with his own mother whenever she disrespected her. Grandmaw was a black saint in his eyes. She even spoke in tongues and laid hands in church. She was a strong black woman. Petite in her upper parts and full figured in her bottom half. Grandmaw stayed "covered". That is prayed up and covered up. She was a young grandmother at just a little over forty-five, yet didn't look a day over thirty-five. She often wore long bright skirt suits and wore her coal black hair in beautiful updo's and ravishing coiling pinups.

Her complexion was like Georgia clay. She had slanted dark brown eyes and long thick lashes. Her eyebrows were perfectly groomed into an imperfect Billie Holiday arch - looking like she shaved them off and drew thin lines above where they used to be. When Grandmaw wore hats, she looked like a young *Mother of the Church* in training. She was originally from Bardstown, Kentucky and a proud & rare "black Catholic turned African Methodist Episcopal" – whatever that means.

Every baby that was born to the family with "good hair" or "funny colored eyes," would evoke stories of Native American & Irish decent. That's how she knew that they belonged to her. She'd say," Mama's baby, Daddy's maybe, but regardless, all ya'lla still be my babies." Disrespecting Grandmaw was like disrespecting God in Raysean's eyes, so he decided to be let him have this one.

"It's getting late, Detective. I have other children to tend to. Is there anything else?"

"Uhhhm, sure, can your grandson give us a description of the woman that he claimed took his friend. Also, a sketch of the car wouldn't hurt," an unmoved Detective Nunnely patronized Grandmaw.

Raysean aggressively stood up from his seat and kicked it up against the wall behind him. Detective Nunnely raised from his chair in defense. Grandmaw held out her arm to restrain the detective. Raysean stomped over to the white board that was on the wall. He picked up a piece of black chalk from the aluminum shelf beneath it, turned it sideways, closed his eyes and his hands took on a life of their own. One hand drew, while the other rapidly smeared. With his back to them, he looked like a conductor of the most beautiful symphony. For the next thirty minutes, Grandmaw, Detective Nunnely, and a room full of investigators watching from the other side of the mirrored glass, were completely mesmerized by the emotional tango of sharp, crisp, short and long strokes.

He turned around with tears in his eyes and black charcoal smeared on his chin and arms with chest heaving - looking like a busy mechanic on a sticky humid day. He backed away to reveal the image that will forever be embedded into his mind. It was a mouth-dropping doppelgänger.

White billowing smoke from new tire peel-out. And in front of it, a gorgeous and one and only make of the four-door Camaro. It was *Night-Rider* black. Wet like latex. It was amazing how Raysean captured the light, shadows and movement into the image. The rims' bling were almost blinding and the wheels seemed to be spinning off the oversized canvas.

It all blended perfectly into the detailed twin of the exotic maroon woman with long dreadlocks pulled up into a gorgeous knot. Her face was the color of rich dark chocolate. Her beautifully deceptive eyes were winking at them all. She was striking. The edges of the carbon copy merged into stormy emotional clouds that filled any free space. The image was a captivating terror.

Detective Nunnely walked over to a hyperventilating Raysean and pulled him into his chest while unclenching his fist from the black muddy chalk. Raysean closed his eyes, gasped and faded to black.

Keenan's drool dribbled down the sleeve of the arm holding up his head. His head slipped, giving him the sensation that he was falling and jarred him awake. His eyes peered around at his surroundings like a paranoid crack head. For a second, he had forgotten that he was in the police station waiting on his cousin and grandmother to come out of that room.

"Damn, did they forget about me?"

An officer walked by gave him a suspicious eye.

Keenan dropped his head, shook it, and thought to himself.

He think he like me jus' cuz he from the hood like me and feel like he "did it", so I ain't got no excuse. He think I don't care about shit. I care about shit. I just don't care about shit that don't care about me. If Ray was here, he'd clown his weak ass.

"Pssss," Keenan scoffed at the curse of being able to hear the thoughts of others.

Leaning back and closing his eyes, he began to doze back off. When he opened them back up, he was sitting courtside of his safe place. He immediately felt relieved. Keenan noticed his basketball in the grass where he left it. He walked over to it and as he went to pick it up, it began to roll. It picked up speed as it rolled down a hill that he had never noticed being there before. He chased his ball down the hill. His body seemed to run faster than his feet and he began to tumble. The tumble gained enormous speed giving him the sensation of *Sonic The Hedgehog.* Keenan slammed into a rocky embankment. He wobbled in his first attempt to stand and checked himself for injuries. He didn't have a scratch on his body. Keenan dusted himself off and searched his surroundings for familiarity. His mouth fell open. Captivated by its breathtaking magnificence, He gazed upon boundless rows of snowcapped mountains. Their peaks reminded him of lemon snow cones, as the morning light reflected against them. A gorgeous valley, adorned by an endless sea of bright colorful flags shimmied between them like a beautifully choreographed Bollywood dance.

He searched around the embankment for his ball and noticed it resting against a small stone. When he got near enough to pick it up, he exchanged his stride for of a creep, just in case. He leaned over to grab it and it began to roll again. It rolled into the choppy cove and was quickly drifting towards dark waters.

In his peripheral, was a figure on the other side of the pristine lagoon. His squinted eyes revealed a tranquil Lotus, dressed in a vibrant white linen salwar kameez ensemble with no shoes. Her salwar was made of a light stretchy material allowing for her legs to be comfortably crossed in *Full Lotus* position and her kameez inhaled and exhaled the soft breeze to the rhythm of the waves that Lotus' eyes were fixated on.

She appeared to be sitting inside of a brilliant egg-shaped ball of light. With her eyes partially open and her head slightly veered to the side, Lotus occasionally shifted her hands and fingers in strange interlocking ways. The longer she sat, the calmer he and his surroundings became. Exotic birds no longer sang, nor flap their wings. And when the rough white waters became as still as glass, she poured her body forward and stretched it out along the rocky embankment before her.

Her hands were outstretched as far as they could reach and formed into a triangle. She then, bent her arms back, folded her hands into the prayer position and touched them to the top of her head, then to the middle of her forehead, and raised to a kneeling position. Her parted eyes revealed the most brilliant of all blues. They looked like aquamarine gems setting against her golden skin.

She then, tapped her folded hands in front of her throat, then to the middle of her chest, next her solar plexus, her navel and finally folded them down in front of her pelvis. Back in standing position, she took a few steps onto the still waters and poured herself out face down again. He watched her repeat these ancient enchanting prostrations all of the way across the motionless elements until she was standing right in front of him. She pulled something invisible from his throat and threw it away, dusting off her hands. She did the same with the middle of his forehead. This time, he felt a slight pull, like a magnet. She

56

repeated the pulling and throwing away motions until he felt a release of pressure. She then drew a symbol in the air above his chest and blew into it. Flashes of his mother on her death bed, memories of being bullied, and the night his father was murdered appeared vivid and transparent in the space between them.

She began to chant in a language that he had never heard before, but understood completely. Her prayer was soft and powerful like the quiet before a perfect storm. She began to shift and interlock her fingers again. Then, she held her fingers up in the blessing mudra and blessed him with complete and utter love. Her fingers resembled Ms. Celie's when she held them up to pass a curse on Mister in the movie *The Color Purple*. Yet, Lotus' intentions were pure and of the highest good. When she passed the blessing of healing and protection over him, the frightening memories that flickered between them burst into an infinite glittery rain of light.

He wept the most ugly, much needed and most unwanted cry.

She smiled.

The whole scenery shook.

"Keenan, wake up, man. Whatchu dreamin' bout that got chu cryin', dawg?"

Keenan's eyes popped open wildly. He was back in the police station.

Back on this ornery ass side.

"Lotus. She's like *sooooomebody*, dawg. We have to find her!" Keenan mustered up through his teary blood shot eyes.

He was having a hard time adjusting back to the heavy vibrations on this plane. His heart and soul ached to be back in the peace and light that they shared. It was a new feel. Raysean extended his hand out to help his cousin out of the chair that he had uncomfortably contorted himself into. When he stood, Raysean pulled him in close and said into his ear, "Yea, dawg. We gon' find her and ets' on errthang."

CHAPTER SIX

STRANGE CLOUDS

The consistent whistle and rattle from the spinning of the ceiling fan with the missing blade - was what finally lulled him to sleep that night. It was also what had awakened him in the witching hours. He glanced at his alarm clock. It read 3:14 AM. He rolled over onto his side and pulled the wavy manila folder from his waist. It was now soft and warm from perspiration and body heat. Wanting, needing to see her face, he slowly and quietly lifted it open with the tips of his fingers.

On the top was a photograph. He fiddled around for his phone and found it under his pillow. Raysean tapped the power button on its side for illumination and held it above the open contents, so that he could see. His heart panged. He felt an overwhelming urge to run and find her now.

Who was she? Where was she? Why was she taken?

His fingertips slowly coursed along her dark fine wavy hair...her deep brown eyes...her bubblegum lips...her kissable chin. He longed for her, needing to caress the space between her ear and neck. Raysean was compelled to pull her close and look her in the eyes with revelation that he had come for her.

Lotus' gut wrenching scream looped over and over, haunting his mind. A tear blinked from his eye onto the 8x10 photograph of Lotus. He smeared it with his shirt. His light went out. Raysean tapped the side his phone again and held the image closer to his face. They were blue, her eyes.

"What's up with that light, Man?" Keenan asked sleepily. Raysean attempted to conceal the picture, but Keenan's dangling head from the top bunk had already seen it. He hopped down and flopped on the bed with his cousin. "Where'd you get that, dawg? Let me see it." Keenan eagerly grabbed the photo.

Raysean gripped onto it, "Don't snatch," he said just before releasing it.

His cousin gazed at Lotus longing to be back in her presence.

Raysean snatched the picture back. "You act like you in love or something," he said jealously.

Keenan snatched it back," You act like that's your girl," he teased back.

"You're stupid, dawg," shot Raysean.

"I had a dream about her." Keenan said grabbing Raysean's full attention.

He always listened to his cousin's dreams. They always came true.

"About what?"

"Her," Keenan responded intensely.

"Come on, Man. You know what I mean...details!"

"Aight...so...it was weird, dawg. She walked across the water...well not *walked* exactly...she was...like...bowing down or some shit...but every time she did it...she was a little closer to me...she kept doing it until she was standing right in front of me...and she wasn't even wet, bruh...it was on some Jesus shit...for real."

Raysean stared at his cousin blank faced for a second. He waited for him to say something else. He hated having to pull information from him.

"And????!!!"

"*And*...She was doing stuff to me."

"Like *WHAT*??!!" Raysean screamed nearly waking the whole house up.

"Sssshhhh!"

"Like what?" he whispered.

"Like...I don't know. She was doing something to me...it was invisible...I don't know...but it felt *real* good." Keenan added toying with his cousin's emotions.

"What did it feel like?"

"I don't know, bruh. Good as hell, though…like the best feeling I ever felt."

"Like a nut?"

"Better than that."

Raysean was mad enough to punch his cousin. There was a hard pause. Keenan heard Raysean's thoughts and felt bad knowing that Lotus wasn't that kind of girl.

"It wasn't like that, cuz. It was way bigger and better than that."

"…and then what?"

"You woke me up."

"What???!!! Think, dawg! She was probably trying to tell you something!"

"That's all!"

"It can't be. Think."

"Her eyes were blue."

Raysean looked at the picture again and turned it around to Keenan. Keenan was astonished.

"Daaaaaayum," was the only thing that Keenan could utter.

They sifted through the papers in the folder for clues to her whereabouts. *Lots of big words. More mumbo jumbo. Numbers. Charts. More pictures.*

"Whoa, wait. Go back!" Keenan said snatching up a few pictures in particular.

Their mouths dropped.

"Hey, where are you two going?" their grandmother asked as they attempted to hurry out of the door five minutes early.

"Skoo," Raysean hastily responded.

The hair on her arms raised up, "School?"

She always attributed the goose bumps to her ESP.

"I told you two, last night, you could stay home, today. The school understands," she said to them with a concerned side-eye.

They attempted to shuffle out of the door when their grandmother called after them again, this time much more stern.

"Raysean Robert Lewis – Keenan Amir Hughes," she said setting her St. Stephen's Woman's Day 2013 coffee mug down on the glass table.

A tsunami of Folgers slightly breached its rim when she stood up. They stopped with their backs turned. She said nothing. She was from the old school and wasn't about to repeat herself again. In unison, they both turned around facing her with their heads to the floor.

"Come here."

They each took baby steps until they reached her.

Simultaneously, she guided them both by the chins and raised their heads up, smearing a dab of grape jelly into the crease of Raysean's mouth with her thumb. She looked her eldest grandsons in the eyes. She wasn't going to lose another child to prison or the grave. Raising her grandchildren were redemption for an early life in the fast lane. In a sense, they were fruit that fell from the tree that she had planted. She had been *around the block* more than a few times, but for some reason, they always seemed to think that she was slow.

"What's the definition of integrity?" she asked them for like the millionth time.

She observed Keenan's lips carefully as he fought off a snickerish grin.

"It's doing the right thing, even when no one is looking," they harmonized.

Raysean's tone drew her attention. It lacked its usual luster. All of her grandchildren held a special place in her heart, but he was her *baby*. She saw a lot of herself in him. His daddy too.

"What's wrong, Ray Ray?" she asked.

He didn't speak, because he knew that if he did, they would never make it out of the house that morning. He just shot her a kind of "you know you don't have to worry about me" look.

"Your sketch, last night..."

Keenan spoke up with a confidence that neither of them had ever seen before.

"Look, Grandmaw. We gotta go. We're going to miss our bus."

Her head involuntarily snapped into his direction. Her face read, "Boy, who do you think you're talking to?" while she quietly admired his new assertiveness. Grandmaw wanted her grandchildren to be strong. She just didn't want them pointing their strengths in her direction.

"Watch who you're talking to. Hurry up, because I ain't driving you to school....*and COME STRAIGHT HOME*!" she yelled after them as they scurried out the door.

She stepped onto her front porch and watched them disappear around the corner in the direction of their bus stop.

The hair on her entire body erected this time. She peered around feeling as though she was being watched. A nippy autumn breeze fondled her intimate spaces. She hugged her housecoat and skipped back into the two-story shotgun style house.

"Ehhhhhh, hold that TARC!" Raysean yelled out to the woman in nursing scrubs.

The cousins sprinted across the intersection briefly halting traffic in both directions. A series of horns and flickering headlights serenated them as they jumped on the 19th and Muhammad Ali bus headed westbound.

An engine started and the tip of the infamous all black everything, four-door Chevy Camaro appeared from the peripheral of some imperfect hedges, and then proceeded in a slow creep in pursuit of the boys.

"Yea, I'm sure this is the house," Keenan replied matter-of-factly to Raysean.

"See?" he asked while pointing up to the wafting smoke stacks hovering above the house, strange clouds.

"Remember we used to think that that factory made the clouds?" Keenan reminisced.

Raysean exclaimed, "Those ain't no muthafuckin clouds! Plus, Grandmaw said that they killed yo' mama," Raysean instantly regretted spewing those words.

Keenan's head slumped at the memory of his mother's death. Raysean shamefully placed his hand on his cousin's shoulder to comfort him. He meant no disrespect towards his favorite aunt, April. Keenan's mom, April, was a councilwoman for the First District and an amazing mother to her children; as well as her brother's children. She was also a tireless activist most notable for initiating the class action lawsuit against the Dewitt Chemical Plant located right in her back yard. She could throw a rock and hit it - the hazardous factory was so close to her home. A week before the pre-trial hearing, Aunt April was admitted into the hospital. Her legs suddenly stopped working. Tests and x-rays revealed a massive malignant tumor on her spine, in addition to, breast and back cancer. She was told that her cancer had already progressed to stage four. She died within four months of discovering the disease. Like a breeze, one day she was here and the next, she was gone.

The beautiful embroidered glass door of The Villages at Park Duvalle home popped open just enough for her face to peek through. Nearly extracting the boys from their skins, she hurriedly yanked them indoors. They shuffled inside. She locked the door behind them and peered through the blinds to be certain that they were not being followed.

"What are you doing here? You have to leave now! It's not safe," Keenan's former foster mother anxiously said to them - totally ditching her Louisville drawl for an English accent.

The boys panned the ransacked house from the dining room. Raysean pulled the folder from his backpack and showed her the picture of her and Lotus' Auntie Qi sitting at a table talking while eight-year-olds' Keenan, Lotus, and Raysean were darting by in the background in, what looked like, a playful game of "it".

"We must hurry! There is little time!"

She motioned them to follow her into the kitchen. They attentively observed her punch in a series of numbers into the oven timer. When she punched in the last number, the oven slid out in front of them to reveal a steep elaborate stairway. They began to follow her down the stairs, and as soon as Raysean's head cleared, the stove began to seal the secret passageway they had entered, leaving them in pitched black. The boys wildly grasped for the shirts directly in front of them. Upon reaching the final twist of the two-story stone walled corridor, a motion sensored light activated and revealed a massive vaulted door.

"This door does not open," she said giving them what would be their first test, while drawing symbols before it.

She glanced over her shoulder, "He that opens this door, meets his maker," the ex-foster mother said before she directly walked through it.

The boys jumped back in amazement. "What tha?!! She just walked through that door!" Raysean exclaimed.

"Hold on, dawg," Keenan replied grabbing Raysean's shirt. "I've seen this door before." Keenan attempted to draw the faint symbol that lay dormant in his sub-conscience. "Move, Man. Let me try," Raysean impatiently asked, not wanting to take the long dark dreadful trek back up the tunnel. The ancient five-tier symbol shone luminously before Keenan.

"I wonder why it's not working. I drew it just like she did," said Raysean.

Keenan couldn't believe that his cousin couldn't see the wondrous illumination glowing in front of their faces. He replied with a baffled expression on his face and then walked through the impenetrable door. Raysean nearly fell on the cold damp floor when Keenan's backpack disappeared through the heavy metal. He tapped it and even took a few steps back to kick it. It was real, yet what he was witnessing was unreal. *This had to be some trick.* He drew the symbol in the air once again, shielded his face and walked through the door.

Raysean was totally amazed by what he saw on the other side. He marveled at over fifty flat screen televisions that filled an entire wall from top to bottom. They captured every angle and every crevice of the dummy house upstairs, it's yard and every house up to the corner of the street.

The room was massive and was the feature of the old dried-up well system that was renovated into a luxury underground bunker.

Raysean nervously spoke telepathically to Keenan," I got a feeling that she ain't who she said she is."

"Yea, me too," Keenan telepathised.

"Very good, boys. You're, right. I'm not who I said I was," the former foster mother said to them as she turned from facing the monitors.

"Quickly! Have a seat. I have much to share in very little time." They sat.

She began to contort and interlock her fingers. As she did this, her thoughts and memories appeared and resounded virtually before them.

"There are many people that seek you. There are those that seek the way to enlightenment and then there are those that seek to extinguish the light. The knowledge that is locked away within you cannot be found in any file, book or scroll. This sacred knowledge is exclusively orally preserved through the divine incarnations of Master Teachers. This sacred knowledge is locked inside of you."

"Speak English, Ms. Melanie?" Keenan interrupted.

"First, my birth name is Jade Lenore, " she responded.

"But, you named me Ana Tinley. It means enlightened sister. I was responsible for your capture and ultimately your self –

immolation. Only your past self and I knew this in the beginning. You hid this truth behind my very eyes. Giving me temporary amnesia was clever enough to conceal my betrayal to The Agency, yet agonizing enough to relinquish my bad karma in this lifetime. I'm so sorry for betraying you, especially after you, not only brought me back to life, but also gave me the gift of eternal life. I owe you my very breath," she breathed heavily.

The cousins shared bewildered glances.

"What the hell are you talking about? What does all that have to do with us right now? How do you know Lotus? Why don't we remember her?! I think that she did something to our memories, cuz! Plus, she lied about her name," Raysean interrogated.

Then, he looked her directly in her eyes and with a balled lip asked," So, all of this was a big ol' lie, huh? How do we know that we can even trust you?"

There were two types of people that Raysean absolutely despised, whores and liars.

"I would never lie to my master," Ana replied falling to her face in a prostration of humility and honor, "I have only followed the instructions given to me, by you, in the final weeks of your last incarnation! The two of you, along with Lotus, are the divine reincarnations of Master Tenzin Lozar Rinpoche. In your past life, you taught me the Silver Veil Mudra and gave me strict instructions to use it the very instance that your incarnations of this life found each other prematurely - that is before your thirteenth birthday."

Raysean absorbed her every word, but most of what she said sounded like "blah blah blah blah blah" to Keenan.

Keenan just couldn't believe that she put her face flat against the floor before them. "That's what Lotus did across the water, dawg," Keenan whispered aloud in complete amazement.

"What do you think it means?" Keenan asked fascinated as he arose from his seat, walked over to Ana and instinctively placed one hand on the crown of her head.

She sat back on her feet in a kneeling position. Her eyes were inflamed from fighting back her tears.

She managed a smile and began to finish," The two of you found each other while still in the ether – the place where we all exist outside of the body when we want to be reborn right away.

Being born as twin cousins provided you with the balance that you so desperately needed in the absence of divine love, or the "Lotus" bud – as that part of you has been affectionately called for ages. And, until you are reunited, you will always yearn for her."

She paused and then continued.

"You first discovered Lotus at the World Fest on the Belvedere when you were only eight. I stopped to talk with a very powerful and gifted woman that we all know very well from your past life. Her name is Kuten Qi and she was and is your kuten in this life, as well as, in the last. I was surprised to see her. She and Lotus were still supposed to be in hiding under the safe refuge of the Drepung Gomang Center. As Kuten Qi neared, I noticed that Lotus was holding her by the hand. My heart skipped a beat when I saw her. I hardly recognized her. She was leaner and taller than she was, at five years old, when I had last seen her. Lotus' shaven head that I had grown accustomed to, flowed with long waist length hair. You two were drawn to her the moment that your eyes connected. Raysean, you walked over to her first. Keenan followed you from closely behind. At first I thought the two of you were going to hug each other, but instead she softly placed her hands on both sides of your face and when she did - her eyes glowed a magnificent blue, then yours, then Keenan's – then random children's in the crowd. We could hear parents starting to take notice as well. Kuten Qi pulled me in close to her. When she touched my arm, flashes from my entire life – even moments that I had no way of remembering – appeared in my mind's eye. I recalled every

70

scene of my life, from waking up that morning to my very conception," Ana recalled.

Then, Ana repeated to Raysean and Keenan, verbatim, what Kuten Qi said to her.

"The master never ceases to amaze me," she said, "What are the odds of his incarnations being split and held amongst rival societies? Nevermind, pupil. We can talk about it at your place, while the children enjoy the rest of their birthday. As long as they're united here, every child in this vicinity that was born under a master number will be instantly awakened. The time for that will come, but that day is not today," Kuten Qi said.

"I know that this will sound confusing, but YOU ARE ONE. By this I mean, all three of you, together; Raysean, Keenan and Lotus. You three are the result of a rare split incarnation. Only those of that are born under the Master Teacher's number are able to perform such a phenomenon. Its main purpose is to elude. It is an action of a Master that..." Ana paused.

"...that does not want to be found," they all said in unison.

"Yes and you gave me, one of your beloved pupils, the grueling task of locating your incarnations. Lotus was discovered in a Shanghai school for super psychic children - the school that you were the head of fourteen years ago. The name of it is The School of Understanding Self or The School of US for short. The founders of this school have very dark agendas for these exceptional children. Lotus was able to flee, with the assistance of the honorable Kuten Qi. This aspect of your incarnation sought asylum in the United States and has lived off the grid here for the past ten years. In your previous life your divinity was contained within a single avatar. Yet, in this lifetime, it is shared within a holy trine - very similar to the trinity of God the Father, the Son and the Holy Spirit. This caused your divinity to be dispersed amongst you all. As individuals, you are capable of anything that you can imagine. But, together, miraculous feats

71

are always within reach. You must be clean in order to find Lotus and it is my responsibility to prepare you. Then and only then will your true divinity be accessible." Ana tried her best to explain.

Suddenly, they all felt a slight tremor under their feet that made them glance at the monitors. Most of them were fuzzy with white noise while the others were filling with smoke and flying debris.

"They're here!" Ana screamed.

Speaking directly to Raysean, she said, "Master, I am addressing you, individually, because one of your many gifts is photographic memory. You see, hear and learn in infinite detail. You don't just see colors, you can hear, smell and taste them, as well. In addition to having six dimensional vision, you also have super empathic abilities. You know what a person is feeling in their innermost core. You know their intent, whether it is positive or negative. Our very lives are dependent upon your super psychic sensitivities to get us to safety. Your primary challenge is to be careful not to confuse another's feelings with your own. It is important to always know the difference. I will help you to remember how to protect yourself."

The buried room rattled again and concrete chunks fell from its ceiling.

"In less than two minutes, a drone will fly overhead and in less than that this whole corner will be obliterated. About a minute afterwards, there will be a "breaking news" report about a gas line explosion and that "three 'unidentified bodies" have been discovered." Ana spoke hurriedly.

Then, she opened an antique trunk with bright red velvet material and flaking wood grain on its sides. Raysean took one look at the trunk and vaguely remembered it sitting next to the fading green zabuton that he had often on sat for days in a meditative state during his past life.

The trunk was filled to its brim with different sized hard and softback books. There were also old scrolls that looked like they would fall apart at the slightest touch. She opened the first book and flipped through its pages.

"Hold on. I can't read that fast!"

"Yea, but you can see and remember that fast. It's not about reading, but more so about taking mental snapshots. You already know everything that I am about to share with you. There is nothing new under the sun. You taught me that," she meekly smiled.

She continued flipping through the first book. It was a Chinese to English translation book.

"Many have died for discovering the people, places and things that I have to show you," she said testing him in Chinese.

"Show me more," he fluently spoke back.

She took two steps backwards and responded," You have less than two minutes to memorize everything in this box. Afterwards, we disappear."

Raysean took one peek inside of the dark tin tunnel and said in a southern drawl, " Hell, naw. I ain't going in there."

He shook his head, sucked his teeth, and stepped back after hearing his resounding utterances bouncing off of the walls of the deep underground passage.

"It's our only way out," Ana responded desperately.

"Why do I have to go first? Shouldn't you go first? You're the adult."

"Master..."

"Raysean," he replied in a tone that rejected his new responsibilities.

"Raysean," she humbly began again. "At this very moment, our survival is dependent upon your heightened abilities of discernment. Let me see your hands." Ana took Raysean's hands in hers and then flipped them over. She applied pressure to the center of each of them with her thumbs. Keenan jumped back after witnessing the brilliant light that shone from his cousin's palms.

Ana continued," Is light emitting from your hands?"

"You can't see this shit?" Raysean replied holding his hands out in front of the entrance of their escape route in complete amazement.

"Good," Ana responded hastily.

Bang! Bang! Bang!

Startled, Keenan snatched and twisted the back of Ana's cashmere shirt as he used her, instinctively, as a shield. Something or someone was attempting to breach the impenetrable door. Keenan trembled and flinched each time that the heavy object collided with the entrance of their fortress.

Bang! Bang! Bang!

Ana struggled to free herself from Keenan's grip, but he was too strong and too engulfed in fear. She focused on her breath and her heart rate quickly began to regulate itself. Ana, then, spoke into his head.

"Keenan, I am not our shield. You are. That door will not hold forever. Now, let me go, please."

He released her from his clutches and they both glanced around for Raysean before lunging for the secret passageway.

Raysean screamed in a loud whisper, "What's taking ya'll so long? Come on!"

He was already about fifty feet ahead of them. Raysean never even looked back. His fight or flight instincts kicked in instantly. Raysean's chest heaved in and out anxiously as he observed Ana peer down the cool dark shaft and pull back. She couldn't see her hand in front of her face. The tunnel was pitched black. Keenan pushed her to the side and peered down the vent to see why Ana hadn't budged. He stood agazed as he witnessed the florescence emanating from his cousin's palms.

Bang! Bang! Bang!

74

Keenan snatched Ana by the wrist, and one behind the other, they pummeled down the ribbed metallic burrow. The secret passageway was about five feet in diameter and was made from thick corrugated steel. Keenan's baby dread locks softly polished the top of the tunnel like a jewelry cloth against an expensive piece. He dusted his hair off with his left hand as Ana tightly clutched his right. Raysean panted as he continued to use his hands as flashlights in a dire attempt to expedite them to safety. His lungs felt as if they were trying to contain the internal fire and intuition that propelled him.

"Cuz, wait up," Keenan yelped as he witnessed his cousin clear a bend in the tunnel. Raysean was now about one hundred feet in front of them. And while Keenan could still see the bright lights that guided them in front of him, it was his inability to see his cousin that freaked him out.

Keenan began to run faster, but the ribs that surrounded the metal tubing tripped Ana up, sending her face first into the cold wavy underground pipeline. Her hands instantly lunged wildly for Keenan's. She began to screech a coagulated scream. It was deep and raspy and seemingly arose from an abyssal crypt or the place where her darkest fears were stored.

She screamed just as he had in the middle of countless nights of nocturnal frights. Ana would sometimes climb into his twin racecar bed with him until he would fall asleep, but more often than most, she would fall asleep as well. It was in that moment, as he was reaching out to Ana's desperately flailing hands that Keenan realized that – Ana was also afraid of the dark.

Keenan extended his hand out to Ana again and this time lifted her onto her feet with just one hard jerk. He exchanged his hand for the back of his t-shirt.

"How much further to we have to go?" Keenan anxiously asked Ana.

"I don't know," she responded.

He began to run again and as he increased his stride he asked," What do you mean, you don't know?"

She panted, "I don't know where we are going. These things are known only by you...the three of you as one. Until you are reunited, we will have to depend upon your individual gifts to guide, ground and protect us."

Keenan stopped just shy of the bend and dug his heels deep into the ridges, stopping them in their tracks. The light from his cousin's palms disappeared into the darkness of the corner he had just turned.

"I can't do this, Ms. Melanie! I mean...I CAN'T DO THIS ANA!"

"But, Keenan, you *HAVE* to."

Keenan began to slump and slide against the curved wall. He hugged his knees when he sat. He was terrified.

"I don't want to fight," he sobbed. "I just want to go home. She told us to come straight home!"

Ana smiled, held the sides of his face and said to her sensai," Aaaahh, there you are. When I was your age, I told you the same thing – that I didn't want to fight. That's when you taught me that a true warrior is one that can prevent war from *even* beginning."

Bang! Bang! Bang!

The two simultaneously glanced back down at the darkness behind them, jumped to their feet and began running again. They ripped around the bend in swift pursuit of the faint and fading glow that was their guiding light. Raysean squinted his eyes and took a deep breath as a crisp breeze and blinding sunlight embraced him.

A trio of fallen leaves engaging in a ménage trios styled merengue skipped across his new *Jordan's* and crashed into the wall beside him. Raysean was amazed at what he saw next.

On the wall was a scribbly written message that read," Keenan was here."

Directly below it was a similar message, "Lotus was here."

Alongside of Lotus' tag was a very different message and in all capital letters, it read, "I AM RAYSEAN."

Beneath his signature was a small handprint traced with black sharpie.

Raysean crinkled his brows wondering how he could be reading a message that he didn't remember writing. Curiosity lured him to hold his hand against the tiny print. Raysean watched his hand dissolve into the wall before him. He quickly drew it back and slowly inserted it again.

Next he slid his head in to see what was hidden on the other side other wall. With his head still on the other side, Raysean dramatically gripped both sides of the wall that the rest of his body resided on and slung his head out. Raysean was totally shaken by what he saw.

BOOOOOOOOOM!

Raysean cringed and whipped his head in the direction of the sound that had just audibly assaulted his eardrums. For a moment, he was relieved to see his cousin and Ana clearing the final bend of the modern day underground railroad. But, his relief was short-lived when he saw the huge fireball that threatened to cremate them.

The heat from the rogue inferno singed Ana's hair. She stumbled and lost her grip from Keenan's hand. Keenan held Ana in his peripheral until his body flipped all of the way around.

Raysean crouched, screamed and awaited the inevitable. Still crouching, Raysean felt a thud up against his back. He turned over to see what had bumped into him and witnessed the most intimidating yet magnificent sight. Both Raysean and Ana had front row seats to the most glorious fireworks that they had ever witnessed. Keenan had both arms stretched out before him and his legs were spread apart into a lunge. He grinded his teeth and squinted his eyes as he held the fire back with his telekinesis. The invisible force propelled the fire giving it the likeness of a wave. The explosives were designed to devour anything and everything that stood in its way. Keenan could only hold the fire back for so long.

Raysean hopped to his feet and then pulled Ana up onto hers. They ran full speed hand in hand into the blinding daylight. Ana, the first to exit, immediately attempted an *about face* as soon as she locked eyes with Saada. Saada rubbed the ganglion scar on her cheek, released her signature crooked smile, and pulled the trigger. Raysean heard three gunshots go off and stopped short of exiting the tunnel. He lost his equilibrium, smashing against and sliding down the dusty piping that beckoned to cradle him.

Raysean recoiled his body and clenched his eyes in anticipation of the inevitable. Behind his palpebra, he saw a vision of a distressed apparition of Lotus squatting in front of him, heavenly and translucent. She gazed into his eyes intensely and dove through the wall where Raysean had traced his hand as a child as if she wanted him to follow her.

Raysean sprung onto his feet. Glancing over his shoulder, he saw that Ana was on his heels. His fingers were outstretched as he desperately grasped for her. Her hand was inches from his when the canon went off. The front of her blouse pooled with red, like dye drops on an Easter egg. She dribbled a bloody smile and collapsed before him.

In a split second, he instinctually knew that he had antecedently cast the Symbols of Intangibility against the wall, as a young child, for that very moment. Without another thought, he dove through the wall.

The symbols were analogous to the intangibility symbols he cast to walk through the thick heavy door of the underground fortress before.

When drawn precisely, and with relevant intent, one could create a permanent or impermanent door before any tangible object.

Keenan allowed the wave of fire to push him back until he was directly in front of the location where he saw his cousin disappear into. He momentarily glanced down at Ana and then, dove sideways through the ghosting door. He emerged on the other side, nose-diving from a steep sixty-foot waterfall that emptied into the Ohio River. Neither he nor his cousin could swim. Keenan closed his eyes and braced for impact.

CHAPTER SEVEN

GATOR

Gator's aged and knotted knuckles bulged when he pulled the worn corded rope until it crackled. Its excess fell against the moss-covered tree he bound it to. The tree had exposed roots that delved deep into the mire.

The old man then lowered his faded camouflaged galoshes back into the shallow murky water. He reached his venous arm into the aluminum boat and fetched his shovel. Gator wore a dingy v-neck thermal with its sleeves rolled up to his elbows and a tattered pair of work pants. He had a stuppled beard, oily salt and pepper hair, and a raised scar above his lip.

Gator thrusted the head of the digging device into the muddy earth using it as leverage to pull himself back up onto the embankment. He slipped when he heard screams and splashes directly behind him.

Gator swung his head around to see someone with flailing arms bobbing up wildly from the bubbling waters. He quickly removed his fishing boots, stood back up, and plunged into the frigid river. Gator could swim like a fish. He swam underwater with the rapid currents. That allowed him to close the distance almost immediately.

Raysean's instincts kicked in and he began wading in the river, as he had memorized from the Navy Seal textbook Ana had flipped through moments before they entered the secret tunnel. Keenan yelped out a cry that singed his throat when he came crashing into the falls alongside of them. Gator submerged himself below the surface like a submarine. He scooped Keenan up and swiftly propelled their heads above water.

Keenan's body was as limp as a wet rag and his eyes were slightly open when Gator laid him down on the damp riverbank. He wasn't breathing. Gator rolled Keenan over onto his side to clear his airways. Thin brownish fluid excreted from Keenan's mouth. He began to cough and then vomit more of the same substance. Keenan's first breath burned his lungs like cool water to a hot pan. His eyes bugged out when he drew in his first breath. Keenan flung his palms out, still in defense against the fireball that had, moments before, nearly consumed them. He panicked and activated his telekinesis and sent Gator sailing through the air.

Gator saw his wrinkled feet above his head as he landed on his back in knee-deep water. A small wave slightly submersed and brushed over Gator's emotionless facial expression. He arose onto his feet, guarding his face with his hands to avoid being struck by the shovel and other flying debris. The boat that Gator had tied to the tree was elevated about six feet in the air, stretching the full length of the rope to its limits.

Surrounding trees began to moan and groan as they bent and bowed as if in honor of the great silent force emitting from Keenan's hands.

Raysean swam, waded and sloshed through cold murkiness until he was standing directly beside Gator.

"Keenan, stop! You're alright, man!" Raysean beamed into his cousin's head to no avail. It was no use. Keenan was in shock.

A flock of blackbirds fled from the top of an old tree that swayed from side to side like Anita Baker in her "Sweet Love" video. Raysean coughed out a congested *verbal* scream, "KEENAN...STOP!"

Keenan dropped his hands and collapsed from overexertion.

The moist Kentucky clay squished between Gator's toes when he climbed out of the water. He reached back and extended his hand out to Raysean and lifted him onto the riverbank. Raysean pushed past Gator and fell on top of his cousin in a fatigued attempt to awaken him.

Gator gently scooped Raysean up.

"What are you doing? Put me down!" Raysean squirmed in resistance.

The old man let out a surly grunt, softly laid Raysean down in the boat, and walked towards Keenan. Gator squatted over Keenan and lifted him up. Gator's legs appeared thin and feeble but they were as strong as an ox's.

Raysean attentively watched Gator lay Keenan down inside the boat alongside him. His mind was running a mile a minute and his chest felt like he had the Mississippi Drumline in it. He began to size the old man up. He was certain that he could take the old rack of bones down if needed, "but for now," he thought," I'll just keep my cool."

"Where are you taking us?" Raysean asked.

Gator started the portable motor.

"Eh, man. Can you hear, dawg? Where are we going?"

When Gator pointed in the direction that they would travel, his weighted down and soggy thermal shirt revealed a black and white tattoo of a bulldog wearing a drill sergeant's hat with the chinstrap attached. Its lower canines resembled sharp horns. The bully dog donned a spiked collar that threatened to gouge into its oversized neck.

"Devil Dog" formed an arch above it and "USMC" in all capital Old English letters cupped the dramatic image from below. *United States Marine Corp* Raysean recalled in his mind from another book that was in the old trunk.

"So, he's a Marine?" Raysean thought to himself.

He cockily entertained himself at the thought of the old man 'trying' him. Raysean recalled, into his mind, the many mixed martial arts books that were in there as well. His mind began to introduce possible scenarios of how to escape unharmed using the knowledge that he absorbed through the sacred manuals and textbooks that Ana flipped through.

Gator steered them to a location about seven minutes away from the Falls of Ohio. He maneuvered the boat through thick aquatic brush that seemed to be never ending. Gator killed the motor and allowed the boat's nose to softly thud against the miniature island. The small landmass was home to dense layers of trees that whistled exquisite melodies as the cool breeze wove through them.

Raysean marveled at a stunning walkway paved entirely of precious stones, fossils and shells. It adorned colorful mesmerizing sequences with spiraling patterns that coiled up to a dome shaped adobe-styled home. The clay abode was made entirely from the earth and recyclable materials. Perfectly manicured herbs and spices grew from its hilly rooftops. To the right of the big arched door, was a strikingly gorgeous window made from the glass bottoms of empty soft drink bottles. When sunlight shone through them, they reflected an emblazoned kaleidoscope that shifted to the rhythmic sways of the trees. Gator hopped onto land and tied up the boat. As he did, a flock of black birds landed into the tops of the enormous Water Maples. Gator slightly tilted his head back and whistled a melodic tune into the air. Surrounding birds echoed a lovely call that swirled all around them.

The sound of the boat rocking from behind interrupted nature's symphony. Gator turned to see both boys standing in the boat. Keenan struggled to regain his balance. He was still weak. Gator extended his hand to him for support as he wobbled onto land. Keenan shivered and shifted side to side as he nervously scoped his surroundings. Raysean pushed Gator's arm away and hopped out of the boat on his on. He didn't want the old man to get it twisted. He could still hold his own if it came down to it. Their eyes and ears honed in on the sound of someone quickly approaching from a shady bend in the distance. The first thing Raysean noticed was that she wasn't wearing any shoes. He thought to himself, *eeeeh, that's nasty*, until he saw her toes.

They were surprisingly soft and clean looking to Raysean, despite the damp cold soil beneath them. Her red-boned phalanges complimented the candy apple polish speckled upon them.

She stepped out of the shadowy brush with a sense of urgency. Her swinging forearms beat her hips like swift palms to an African drum. She wore a pink bodice over a floral symmetric bohemian styled skirt. Its long tattered and frayed trail quickly slithered along the earth behind her.

She stopped before them and began to rapidly clap her hands.

"Hurry up! Take your shoes off!"

"What?" Keenan scoffed, "It's colder than a pimp out here."

"I ain't taking my J's off," Raysean reinforced.

The sound of a helicopter's propellers beat in the nearby distance. Their eyes all nervously shot up towards the greying skies.

The cousins annoyingly glanced at each other before stepping out of their sneakers using their heels against their toes. They never ever walked barefoot. It makes your feet fat and you could get a hookworm in them. That's what Grandmaw said, atleast.

"Socks, too," she snapped over her shoulder as she swiftly walked away. No matter how much she'd longed for visitors, she was still particular in her ways.

The boys reluctantly followed her orders. It wasn't like they had much of a choice.

Raysean did a quick scan of her energy. Strange. She seemed to have been expecting them.

"And your clothes," she yelled as she neared the hidden home. Their bodies nervously stiffened.

"That didn't come out right," she thought to herself.

She burst out in laughter when she turned to see Keenan reluctantly beginning to remove his shirt.

"Not out here. There!" She said with a rasp.

Her words sounded like a jazz musician beebopping to a sassy percussion. She teasingly pointed in the direction of the bend from which she had come.

"Gator, take these boys and get them out of those wet clothes. After that, prepare a boil." Gator nodded in agreement.

White sage overpowered their senses when Raysean and Keenan entered the den of the hidden dwelling. It was cool, cozy and chic. The wavy walls' had small grooves that were home to more than one hundred handmade candles and scented oils that emitted the most delectable fragrances. Each wall also had large curves that extended out resembling brilliant sunlit sand dunes. On one wall, was a uniquely sculpted chaise lounge. On the other two, were smoothly carved sofas.

The teens' shadows waltzed around the illuminated clay walls, grasping her attention. "Wait," she said.

She turned and lifted her burning smudge stick from the clay bowl that it was smoldering in. "Hold your arms out."

Raysean and Keenan were willing to do anything to sit close by the warm fire that crackled in the room behind her. She waved the white sage around their fronts and backs, as well as, around their arms and under their feet. It resembled rolled tobacco secured by a single strand of twine that spun from the bottom to the top. The dried leaf felt like satin to the touch and gave off a robust spicy aroma.

They coughed when they walked through the thick white smoke that wafted around them. She laughed.

"What's up with all the smoke?" Raysean asked.

"It clears negative energy. It was my job to do it to *everybody* that would come to our house. White folks, black folks, creole folks, cajun folks – all kinds of peoples, came from all around to see Muh'Dear." The young girl stared out into space for a moment, batted her eyes and then changed the subject.

"Ya'll boys hungry?"

Keenan gave a weary look to his cousin, "She crazy as hell," he beamed.

Raysean nodded a yes to the both of them, then nervously asked their host," How long will it take for our clothes to dry?"

It was something very strange about this girl and the old man that just happened to be in the right place at the right time. Why were they so eager to help them? It wasn't every day that white people rescued them from the river and then invited them over for dinner. Raysean couldn't put his finger on it. He just knew that people haven't been who he thought they were lately. Ms. Melanie wasn't really Ms. Melanie. She was really Ana. And who was Ana, really? Why were bad things happening to everyone around him?

"Gator, we're ready for supper," the girl called out," aw, and it's going to take a while for your clothes, but you're welcome to make yourselves at home. Unless, you plan on sloshing away in those soggy sneakers and those dingy old work clothes."

She wanted so desperately to blurt out the truth, the truth about expecting them, but decided to wait until after they all ate. She would ease the truth about her talents to them as the night neared.

Raysean took one look at the large patch sewn on his knee and knew that he wouldn't last one second on public transportation in his current attire without confrontation. He knew that somebody would eventually provoke him.

"How long is a while?" Raysean asked crinkling his brow and crossing his arms.

"As long as it takes. It's not like you got a whole lot of options." She really wanted be bold enough to say that, but she couldn't. She needed them to trust her first. She didn't want to scare them off with her "hocus pocus". She decided that it was best to just take her time.

Instead she said, "Tomorrow afternoon, worst case. I'll have Gator hand wash them after dinner and set them out to dry, but it's chilly out."

"Tomorrow afternoon is more than enough time to lay everything out on the table," Red hoped.

Raysean panicked.

"Tomorrow afternoon? We can't wait that long. You got anything else that we can put on?"

"Bruh, what are you thinking?" Keenan gripped his cousin by the elbow and whispered into his ear," We can't take this heat to Grandmaw's house! People getting murked, dawg!"

Raysean lowered his eyes and began to rapidly rub the sides of his head in frustration. He knew that Keenan was right. He wasn't thinking clearly.

Thoughts of his last moments with Ana flooded his mind. Raysean knew that she was dead. He saw it in her eyes. She was dead before she even hit the ground.

If he couldn't save Ana, how could he save Lotus? He just wanted to go back to the place in time before Lotus screamed his name. Her sultry shriek, terrifying and pure, echoed between his ears.

The young girl sensed Raysean's defeat and interrupted it with a soft stroke to the side of his face. She gasped when he lifted his head and their eyes met. Her eyes were as dark and deep as a well, yet were as bright and wishful as an innocent child's. Her soft sandy coils, bouncy and full, fell into her face. She tussled her hair and revealed a shiny tan scar on her temple. Raysean felt the urge to course his thumb gently across it. For a moment, he felt that she could really see and understand him.

She parted her lips to speak, but nothing came out.

"I think that we need to chill for a while until we can figure out a plan. How much stuff from Ana's trunk do you remember?" Keenan asked.

"Everything. I just need to figure out how it all goes together."

"I know you, bruh. You can figure this shit out easily."

"He's right. Maybe all you need his something hot on your stomach to get your wheels churning. The food smells ready," she winked her eye, "I don't know about you, but I'm ready to hurt something."

They followed her into the room one after another.

Raysean noticed Gator staring at them intensely as he awaited them by the fireplace. "Why don't your granddaddy talk?" he asked.

She smiled and leaning on one hand, she propped herself up as she sat softly with her legs to the side. She attentively watched Gator stir the steamy contents in the cast iron pot that hung above the flame. Its aroma caused her to salivate.

Corn on the cob, crawdads, potatoes, onions, bay leaves, butter, garlic and shrimp were just some of the items she spotted in the aromatic swirl.

"That smells real good, Gator. This might be your best pot yet," she said.

As Keenan and Raysean sat down beside her, she continued, "He ain't my granddaddy. I ain't got no family. The end."

Raysean wrinkled his brows and asked," Who is he then?"

"He ain't my sugar daddy if that's what you're thinking."

"I wasn't thinking that!"

"Yea you was, dawg," Keenan joked.

The young girl imitated a southern bell accent when she said, "Where *are* my manners? She glanced at the old man and said, "We were so excited to have guests that we skipped the introduction *all* together."

She extended a seated cursty to each of them and said in an exaggerated hood accent, "I'm Cayenne, but you can call me Red. I think that's how this usually works," she said making a loud popping sound with her mouth.

Keenan laughed his name aloud.

"Ray," his cousin said managing a side grin.

Red held out her arm and said," And, this is Gator, my slave."

Gator groaned at his introduction as he lifted a tarnished silver spoon to her mouth.

Red cautiously slerped hot broth from the spoon that Gator ladled against her pink puffy lips. She licked them, leaving a thin glossy glaze, wincing as she endured pain for pleasure.

The boys wiped their smiles from their faces.

"Slave?" Raysean was taken aback by her answer.

"For real?" Keenan asked eyeballing the pot.

Raysean didn't need to ask. He could feel that she wasn't kidding.

"Yesss, for real," she sassed, "and if you knew what his family did to my family, you wouldn't have one bit of compassion for him."

"Nah, for really though?" Keenan asked.

Red replied with a blank faced stare.

"Make him do something then," Keenan instigated.

"She been making him do shit all day, dawg," Ray intervened,

"How much proof do you need, bruh?" Raysean knew that she was serious. He'd been scanning their energy since their arrival. Despite her sarcasm, he knew Red was "cool peoples".

It was Gator that was as hollow as the branches on a dead tree. All Raysean could get from him was shade. He recalled his bones creaking like old stairs as Gator carried him to the boat, yet his strength was unwavering.

"What do you mean by slave? Can't he leave if he wants to? What did his family do to your family?"

Red defensively asked, "How did you fall out of the sky?"

"How did you know that we fell out of the sky?"

"Your turn!" Red wasn't budging.

"Ooooowwwweeeee! That white girl's fiesty, bruh," Keenan instigated.

"You ain't going to believe it. I don't even want to believe it," Raysean said.

"White girl?" She glared at Keenan," Boi, I can trace my roots all of the way back to Africa, and you probably don't even know your daddy, so slow your roll and know your roll, baby."

Red would always go for the jugular when she felt attacked or fronted, contrary to what she was taught. Being classy. Being a lady, was constantly emphasized by all of her family members. She turned her attention back to Raysean, "Tell me."

Raysean hesitated. Keenan blurted out, "We jumped through an invisible door! Aye, can you put some of that juice on the spoon for me too?"

Red's eyed bulged. Raysean mugged Keenan in the side of his head. Gator looked to Red for approval to give Keenan a taste of the steamy juice. She nodded an irritated yes.

"What? Invisible door? Really? How?"

"Your turn."

"Um, yea, slave," she shot back defensively.

"Ball's back in your court."

Keenan moaned in ecstasy and cried out, "Oh my God, nigga, what is this soup called? It's thuuuuuunda!"

Red rolled her eyes, "It's not soup. It's a boil, boi. Ya'll want to just eat first and ask questions later?" She impatiently asked.

Gator scooped up the steamy ingredients into a large bowl with a built in strainer and held it above the pot. He then poured the contents of the bowl into a newspaper-lined metal bucket. Steam rolled above it like volcanic ash.

Keenan picked up a crawdad that fell from the container and pretended like he was going to make it bite Red.

She smacked his hand and asked, "Where yo manners?" She closed her eyes.

He wrinkled his brows and raised his shoulders in a clueless expression.

Raysean telepathically said to him, "Pray, dawg."

Keenan closed his eyes, grinned and began in a mock preacher voice," *Lord, thank you for this food that we are graciously about to receive.*

Ahe

Bless this food for the nourishment of our bodies.

Ahe

Dear Lord, you bless us in our rising up and our goings down.
asha lala mamase mamasa mamakusa heee heee heee"

Raysean frogged his cousin in the thigh, "Stop playing, dawg. Grandmaw told you about playing with The Lord like that."

Red burst out into an uncontrollable laughter. She cupped her hands over her mouth to hide the sliver of space between her top front teeth. She hadn't been around anyone her age for a very long time.

"What's wrong with you, boi? Are you really this retarded!"

Keenan held his face to hold his giggles in, but it was no use. It only made him make a snorting noise that provoked them all to fall out into another round laughter.

Eventually, they all sat up and agreed to eat their food before it went cold.

After a few moments of finger-licking, slurping and smacking, Red broke the silence. In a serious tone, she said, "I think that I may be able to help you. You know - find the girl that you looking for?"

"How you know about, Lotus?" Raysean asked eagerly.

Red looked up intently," Is that her name? I saw her when I touched your face."

Ray felt his face begin to warm and his heart rate pick up. "What did you see?"

"I *saw* them take her. I *felt* you lose her." Red's eyes welled.

"Go on." Raysean needed more, so much more.

"I can see why you like her so much. She's beautiful."

"I knew that you liked her," Keenan blurted out and punched Raysean in the shoulder.

"Who the fuck *are* you and how you reading my mind?" Raysean asked defensively.

Red rolled her eyes and spoke through her teeth," This is my house, so please don't disrespect it with your nasty mouth. Loose lips sink ships, baby, "she eerily responded.

Raysean could sense her energy shifting, despite the smile that she masqueraded. He could feel her anger building up. He could tell that she wasn't the type that made threats. She made promises. Red was a lot like him.

"What my cousin is trying to say is," Keenan cued as he looked over at Raysean.

"My bad for cussing, but..." Raysean began.

"It's okay," she said. She was reading him as well. Red could feel that whatever he was about to say – anything that he would ever say, would be real. He had her at - "My bad..."

In her thick creole accent she answered Raysean's question," I'm from New Orleans, born and raised, *baby*. I'm the only living survivor of the Lenore family and until you two got here, me and Gator was the only ones that knew it. I am the great great granddaughter of the infamous voodou queen, Mama Lenore. They say that I am a splitting image of her. Kind of hard to believe that there was another as light as me, especially, with me being as white as sliced bread in a family dark as burnt toast. And for no reason at all. You couldn't see my mama or daddy at night. I figure, if I come from a line of queens, then so am I."

"So, basically you're a witch?" Keenan asked.

"I ain't no witch, *baby*, and ain't nothing basic about me," Red snapped.

She leaned in, "That little trick that you did by the river was cute, but I guaran-damn-tee you that there ain't a queen or witch alive that can take a look at me."

"Prove it!" Keenan asked instigating again.

"Prove what?" Red asked.

"Do something to make us believe you. What can you do?" he replied.

"I can make you love me," she smirked.

Raysean smiled and said, "Do it."

He wanted to see if she was the real deal, before they shared their secrets with her.

"I don't think that you know what you're asking for. Have you ever loved someone or something that was not certain to love you back?" she asked in a serious tone. Raysean's heart weighed heavily as the thoughts of his mother entered his mind. He knew what it was like to, not to only want, but to so desperately need his love reciprocated. He also knew what it felt like to have his heart shattered into infinite pieces from her neglect. If being in love was anything like that – Raysean wanted no parts of it. That was until he laid his eyes on Lotus.

Raysean blinked his eyes to snap back to reality. He re-focused his eyes to see Red working some sort of trance over Keenan. She touched the bottoms of each of his feet saying, "I am the ground beneath your feet. Take your root up in me – daughter of sacred Mama Earth."

Keenan snickered and shook his head, "Corny," he thought to himself.

Then placing her hands into his she continued," When you are weak, I will be your strength – always."

Lastly, she balled up her fist and knocked on his chest above his heart. "When I knock, you will open up to me – always."

She then leaned in and gave him a surprise pop kiss. It was the first for both of them. When she sat back on her knees, she noticed that his eyes were still closed and his lips still puckered. Raysean began to laugh aloud. "Are you serious, dawg?"

When Keenan opened his eyes, everything appeared much more vivid – but besides that he hardly noticed any change.

"It didn't work. Kiss me again," Keenan said.

"Taste that corn," Red said to him.

He picked up the half ear and bit into it. Warm buttery juice bursting from mowed kernels exploded onto his taste buds. It was sweet and salty and for a moment he thought that he could even taste yellow. Every tender morsel was the best he'd ever had.

"Damn this is some good ass corn," Keenan said with his mouth full and greasy and ecstasy dribbling down his chin.

"Nah, *baby*. That's love," Red clarified. "Everything is better when you put a little love in it. Ain't that right, Gator?"

Gator grunted in agreement.

"Boooooo," Keenan dismissed, "That was weak. Do something else."

Red narrowed her eyes at him. Keenan flashed his dimples and blew her a kiss," You a cute lil' white girl when you mad."

"And as cute as you are, you workin' my nerves. Sleep," she said impatiently as she swiped her palm in a downward motion.

Keenan fell on his side like a sack of potatoes.

"He always this annoying?"

"Only when he *really* likes you," Raysean joked. She blushed.

Red held her hand up to awaken Keenan, but Raysean stopped her.

"Before you wake him back up – Lotus, tell me about Lotus. What did you see?"

"I saw that you are the one, the only one that will rescue her."

"How do you know that? Tell me what you saw?"

"I saw you running with her hand in hand, and when ya'll ran, the earth trembled beneath your feet."

"What else?"

"I only stroked your face for a second."

"If you saw all of that just by touching me for one second, how do I know that you're not making this all up?"

"Because – you know," she said as she stared intensely into his eyes. "I have something that I need to show you."

"What is it?"

"I can show you better than I can tell you," Red said as she flipped her palm over to swipe upwards in preparation to awaken Keenan.

"Let him sleep," Raysean whispered prodding her to agree.

"Okay," she spoke softly.

Red raised in one motion from a seated position. Her bottom shook like two moroccans when she brushed the back of her skirt off.

"Gator – the clay. Bring the clay." Gator hung his head low.

"Tell me that you didn't forget my clay. How am I supposed to finish now?"

"Is that what the shovel was for? Shid, I thought that you was going to kill us and bury us with it," Raysean jested to Gator. Gator's face was expressionless.

"He always this weird?"

"He's not ever going to talk to you. Trust me. It's been just me and him for a long time. He's loyal. He's obedient. But, he don't talk. He can't. He's dead."

Raysean's face crinkled. "Dead dead?"

Red smirked. "As a doorknob. Come on. I'll tell you on the way." She spoke sternly to Gator, "It's the blood moon and I'll have to wait a whole 'nother year for that clay, if I don't get it tonight. So, guess who's gonna make sure that that don't happen? Go on. The falls are probably swarming with police by now. So, you need to be more careful than ever. I'll cloak you, but your steps still need to be light as a feather. If there are search dogs, they will definitely catch your scent. So, be careful Gator, and hurry up. A bucket of mud should be more than plenty. Be good." Gator nodded.

Red grabbed a candle from one of the wall pockets and lighted their way through a narrow cobblestone passageway that sloped until it emptied into a lavish indoor cellar.

Fresh scents from a wide array of botanical organics filled the air. His senses danced to the euphony of water trickling continuously from holes cut into interconnected hollow canes that hang from the ceiling. Directly below were root vegetables of nearly every kind growing in large pots made from old wine barrels. On the walls, were wooden shelves that stored a colorful array of glass jars filled with delicious preserves, vegetables and ground spices. Raysean was captivated by the lush garden that was grown and stored from below.

Red jumped back into the conversation feet first.

"Story goes, Mama Lenore let out a bloodcurdling curse on Gator's great grandfather the night that he ripped her screaming son from her grips. She cursed her slave master. She cursed him good too. She wailed something like this...

Vincente Pierre, I curse you! I curse your sons! May the gates of Hell open up and swallow you up alive. Hell won't wait for your death. Oooooh, you, your sons, and your son's sons will know what it's like to be swallowed up whole! He kicked her off of the leg that he was dragging her by and said something like, *"Heifer, he's sickly anyway. He won't be no use round' here, no way.* That night, Vincente Pierre tied my eighteen month old distant uncle by the ankle to a bush on a bank not far from a alligator's den."

"I don't want to hear no more," Raysean interrupted.

"Baby Russell cried as he tugged away from the bush trying to free himself. That's when the alligator came out. They say the gator did a little happy dance as if he was wobbling over to a favorite delicacy. Slaves that witnessed it said that he didn't swallow baby Russell whole like Vincente Pierre said. They said that the alligator chomped down on the baby's torso and his tiny little arms and legs dangled from the sides. They said you could hear the baby whimpering all the way up until the alligator submerged into the water. The entire time, Vincente Pierre was yelling... *What are you waiting for? Shoot him! Shoot him, son!* When Master Pierre's son aimed the shotgun's nozzle at the alligators head, he lost his balance and fell in. The young Pierre was just twelve years old when two gators tore him from limb to limb. That night Vincente Pierre charged into the slave quarters dragging Mama Lenore and all of her children outside. Master Pierre busted in mad screaming...*You take my son, you nigger bitch? Then, I'll take all of yours! String them up!*" Vincent Pierre hang four of Mama Lenore's sons while her and her daughters begged for him to stop. The next morning, Master Pierre found Mama Lenore hanging right beside her sons. Witnesses said that her last tear-flavored words were – *not another drop of my sweet warm milk will fill yo babies' bellies...not another wretched drop.* Mama Lenore had cared for and breastfed all of Master Pierre's children, including his infant son, Georgie, who also died right after that. Fast forward to a few years back, Muh'Dear took me into town with her to take care of some business, she said. We went inside of the bait store. As soon as we walked in, she got into an argument with the man behind the counter. I remember her demanding him to take the things down off the walls and out of the cases. She said that it was disrespectful to her family. He kept telling her to leave or buy something."

"*You going to buy something or not, gal?*"

"*I wish the hell I would buy something out of this hell hole! I hope that it burns like yo granddaddies.*"

"*Leave now, you nigga witch!*"

"He pulled out a shotgun from behind the glass case and pointed it at her. She didn't blink an eye, but she tensed up when he pointed it at me, though. He lowered it to my face and used the nozzle to clear my hair from my eye. Then he said...*Ain't you a cutie? You remind me of the little guhl I always wanted. Here, hold out your hand, I got something for you.* Muh'Dear put the same fake smile that she used to put on for Jehovah's Witnesses when they would knock on the door...*Not today, she said politely. Maybe another time, Cayenne.* That's when Gator reached under the counter and handed me a miniature doll that fit into the palm of my hand. It was a figurine with a bobbling head of a black baby crawling in a diaper. It had big red lips and even bigger eyes. I'll never forget what he said after that...*Gator bait for Gator bait* he laughed like a nasty old man. Muh'Dear pulled me in close to her and asked him, "*You know you a little old for a man in your family. Sure you family?* Her words stunned him and we got out of there real quick! Muh'Dear shut him down. He realized in that moment that she somehow knew that he was adopted. Muh'Dear figured out that that's why Mama Lenore's curse didn't work on him. That night was the first night that Muh'Dear and I practiced voodou together. I was so excited to be allowed to do more than just wave smoke around people. She drew symbols onto the floor and sat the gator bait bobble head doll in the center of them.   Her next words will stay with me forever...*Daughter, people take swords with them to war, but the Lenore women, we take voodou. It is our rite of passage, but you, my grandest daughter, are different. You don't need a book of spells or magic. You are the spell. You are the magic. The light and the darkness both await your every beck and call. Every word that spills from your lips is a spell. The only difference between a blessing and a curse is your intention. Do you understand, daughter? I think so,*" I told her.

Raysean hung on to Red's every word.

She continued to share her family history with him.

"Then Muh'Dear said...*You also have something called immunity. Do you know what that is, sweetheart? No...*I told her. I had never heard the word before in my life...*It means that no spell or curse can harm you...Your mother's photo from the mantle, hand it to me.* When I passed her the picture of her only child, she withdrew her hand and let it to fall to the floor. Tiny pieces of glass splashed against our feet. My heart sank. I asked her...*Muh'Dear, why would you do that?* Her response was...*I'm sorry, daughter. Please forgive me.* I told her that I forgave her, but really I was never more confused. Then, Muh'Dear looked down at the broken glass and asked me...*See how my apology* *didn't piece the frame back together? In the same way, you will not be able to undo your spells or curses. So, speak wisely. Speak wisely, daughter.* Then, I asked Muh'Dear...*Did his great grandfather really own us?* And she said...*Yes, baby. Mama Lenore and many others were not even seen as human beings. That's why they put us down as property, right there next to the farm animals and equipment.* I was pissed, so I got mad and said...*He should know what it's like to be a slave too. Maybe then, he won't treat black people like that.* That's when she said to me...*Hush, child.*" She said in her best imitation of Muh'Dear. Then Red began again.

"I passed my first and only curse that night, because I didn't like the way that I felt on the inside afterwards. I can't describe it, but I wasn't myself. I lusted all night at ideas of torturing this man. And check this out, Gator died in his sleep that night. The coroner said it was a heart attack, but when his landlord found him, his mouth and eyes were wide open like something scared him to death. The day after his funeral, I woke up to him standing at the foot of my canopy bed. He was wearing a dusty military uniform. I was scared to death when I first saw him, so I screamed at the top of my lungs, and so did Gator. He continued to scream even when I stopped. Muh'Dear barged into my bedroom. She probably thought that somebody was trying to kill me. She hollered...*What the hell?* She took one look at Gator screaming bozerk and said to him...*Shut up, you old fool!* Gator continued to scream. Muh'Dear put her hands on her wide hips and said to me...*This here is your doing! You said that he should know what it feels like to be a slave, so here you go, you got yourself a slave. Now, tell him to shut up, so that I can go back to bed.* I let out a squeak...*Shut up!* And, he shut up for good. He grunts from time to time, but that's about it."

"Damn! Now, I see why you're so sensitive about words." Raysean said.

Red stopped talking when they came upon a wooden table. It had three little clay figures and a little boat that was tied to a tree on it. One of the figures was cradling the other, while the other lay in fetal position inside of the vessel.

"What is this? Is this us?"

"Yes. I sculpted smaller versions of all that you see, this house, this cellar, so that Gator will have a clear idea of what I wanted him to build. The other day, I intended on making a bowl, but instead, zoned out. I swear, I could feel you two. My fingers began to mold you and the scenery until I ran out of clay. There's a lot more sculpt. I think that this is how we can find out what happens next."

"We? You make it sound like we a team. I don't think that you understand what's going on out here. I don't even understand. All I know is that, yesterday morning, my life completely changed. Shit's crazy out here in these streets, mane."

"You make it sound like I have much of a choice."

"What do you mean?"

"Watch this. Yesterday was the first day that I realized that I could do this."

Red held her hand above the display and began to swirl it in a spiraling motion, until they could both see the subtle spirals. They expanded until they rippled into the atmosphere.

"Life," she spoke softly.

The figures rewinded as they came to life. The boat began to rock wildly against the waves. A mud figure standing on the bank appeared to be the culprit. Raysean watched in awe as each scene played back (from them crashing into the river to their arrival at Red's place) exactly as it occurred.

"Damn. What happens next?"

"I don't know, but I got a feeling that we're stronger together. I wasn't able to do what I just did, until I could feel ya'll. I could feel ya'll like I can feel my own skin." Red caressed her fair skin. It's summer tan was quickly fading.

"Now that you say that, we all did some things that we weren't able to do before today. I think you right about us being more powerful together. Maybe we need to find the others."

"There are others?"

"Yeah, it's a whole lot of us in the United States, but way more in China."

"How many?" Red's insides did somersaults at the idea of others like them.

"Thousands."

"Oh, My God! That's crazy...to have friends...I mean...to have friends just like me."

"How long have you been alone?"

"What do you mean? I'm not alone. I have Gator," she asked with her head lowered.

She wasn't about to let them in, when all they would do was leave. They all left her. Everyone. Katrina sucked them up like heads off crawfish and spit them out floating into the canals.

"I mean, how long have you been without your family?"

"Since I was five going on six."

"How old are you now?"

"About to turn sixteen."

"You've been living on your own for almost ten years?"

"How old are you?"

"Me and Keenan, we both fourteen, and like you say, "going on" fifteen. We even got the same birthday."

"Twin cousins," she smiled.

"Yea. We more like brothers, though."

Red froze in place. Her eyes stared out into a hazy gaze. Raysean grabbed and shook her by the forearms.

"Red, you aight?"

"It's Gator. He's in trouble."

"How do you know?"

She raked her fingers through her springy sun streaked hair, "The little birdies just told me."

Gator had parked the boat not far from the site where he rescued Keenan and Raysean. He hopped out and began to trek the rest of the way. As he neared the final tree, he set his bucket down. He attentively watched Coast Guard comb the area with its spotlight. The searchlights resembled the beginning of Thunder Over Louisville, the world's largest fireworks display.

Dead and dying leaves rain down on Gator's head. He looked up to see that the blackbirds had landed into the tops of the trees. They were Red's eyes. She always sent them to watch over Gator. Each bird gave her its own view and perspective. Her vision became better than a hundred compound eyes.

It wasn't much that she missed in the city. She literally had a bird's eye view of every outside event or person that she wanted to observe discreetly. Red loved to people watch and had an attraction to both boys and girls, but particularly boys.

Gator looked up and let out a sigh of relief. He knew that as long as she was watching him she would not let anything bad happen to him. She was still the only face that he remembered from his past. His worst fear was to wake up buried again.

He waited until the Coast Guard moved further upriver before he cleared the trees. Gator began to dig into the stone-cold soil with his fingers and hands throwing the dirt to the side. After about three feet deep, he noticed a change in consistency. He had just struck clay. Gator began to fill the pail with rich Kentucky clay. He was waist deep by the time that it was full. He pulled his upper body from the hole that he had dug, raised to his feet and prepared to head back. The clouds took up their anchor and an autumn breeze sent them sailing across the dark skies.

The moon's glow casted a misty spotlight onto a black panther crouching in a thicket. Its nocturnal eyes glowed a fluorescent silvery-grey. Gator stopped walking abruptly and the pail squeaked back and forth in mid air.

The black cat dug its hind legs into the earth as it prepared to lunge. It wore a glorious leopard coat of shiny spotted silk. It steadied before leaping towards the floating bucket and knocking Gator to the ground. Gator swung the heavy bucket and hit the cat in its nose. It painfully pawed its face. When Gator attempted to get free, it pounced on him with its enormous mitts. Its claws dug deep into Gator's cold rubbery flesh. A dark gooey substance seeped from his gaping wounds. Gator groaned in agony.

Above and all around them, birds exploded from the trees. They looked like seeds bursting from black dandelions. Thousands of them swarmed the exotic feline, using their beaks as tiny spears. The cat cowered low to the ground to end the torturous ripping and tearing. It hissed and bear its vicious canines as it searched for Gator below the horde of flying darts. Black feathers and dark puffs of fur fell down on him when he scrambled on to his feet. Sharp beaks tore into the flesh of the big cat as it pinned the silhouette of Gator to the ground.

The cat wildly scratched and clawed as it animated and morphed into a naked woman with skin as rich as molten chocolate. Her dreadlocks, full of life, grew long and thick as they cascaded, clung to, and covered only her intimate places. Saada arched her back and inhaled above Gator's chest. She clutched her throat as she began to choke and gag. She started to dry heave when the second tide of black birds came rapidly rolling in. Saada screamed as they spun her around wildly, shearing her skin. She quickly shifted back into a panther and leaped off into the brush. As Gator tore through the trees, vague images of him running through a dense forest as bullets zipped past him, flashed before him. He ran harder. Faster. His bare feet pounded dark coagulated impressions into the slippery leaf covered ground. He dove into his boat and started its motor. He turned to see the big black cat staring intensely at him from the mouth of the bank.

"Gator! You okay? Gator!" Red screamed as she hugged and pelted Gator in the chest. "Don't ever scare me like that again! I thought...I thought!" She noticed the claw marks in Gator's shirt and panted, "Oh, my God, Gator, you're hurt! You're bleeding!"

"That's blood?" Keenan asked interrupting all of the commotion.

"I don't do blood," Raysean said.

"Shut up and help me!"

Keenan supported Gator on one side while Raysean supported him on the other.

"Peeeeuuuuu! He's foul, bruh." Keenan said.

"He's dead, dawg. What's he supposed to smell like?" Raysean asked.

"Dead?" Keenan withdrew his support from Gators arm.

"Boi, you from the hood. Don't act like you ain't never seen the walking dead before. Hand me that bucket and lay him down right here," Red impatiently replied to Keenan.

She opened Gator's shirt and revealed a ghastly wound across his chest. Red rubbed some of the cold auburn clay into Gator's gaping pectoris. She held her hand above his injury and the salve spread and thickened into a hideous keloid scar. Red wiped a tear from her cheek, smiled and regained her composure, "You do reek of death. Go clean yourself up," she said.

Gator stood and helped Red onto her feet.

Keenan asked, "What in the hell did I miss when I was sleeping?"

"Get the bucket, boi, and come on. We'll catch you up on the way. We don't want whatever that attacked Gator to attack us," she sassed as her eyes searched the night sky.

"Damn, et's deep," Keenan smiled after hearing the nutshell version of the story about Gator and Red, as well as, a summary of the clay figures that came to life.

His dimples appeared bottomless.

Red took a deep breath and then closed her eyes as she entered a trance-like state. She poured water into her palms allowing it to seep into a hole that she had molded in the middle of the clay. Red, first, shaped a mound and allowed it to slip through her fingers as she tapped the pedal that spun the round table with her foot. She then, set aside four smaller mounds and sculpted mini versions of each of them. Next, Red molded what appeared to be a clash between the police and a group of people.

"Life," she spoke as she rotated her palm in a clockwise spiral above her creations. The scenes that played out left them all speechless.

CHAPTER EIGHT

RUN NIGGA RUN

Keenan awakened to deep emotional humming. He couldn't make out the song, but it was as soulful as The Jefferson's theme song that played at the end of each episode. He peered through Red's thick curly ringlets that obstructed his view. She lay comfortable, snoring, and drooling on his chest. He blew her hair, so that he could get a good view of the full figured woman that was leaving the room. Keenan eased Red's head from his chest and escaped her quiescent clutches. She whimpered and snuggled into the oversized comforter that they all shared. It was made from hemp material and was triple stuffed with goose feathers. Keenan glanced over at his cousin and laughed to himself. He had a death grip on those covers. *Cover thief.*

He searched the room for Gator and found him standing as stiff as a board by the fireplace just as he had been hours before. He didn't appear, in the least bit, drowsy. They exchanged weird expressions and Keenan continued to follow the closed-lip singer into a room that he hadn't noticed was there before. It was fully furnished with antique furniture and ceramic Africa themed knick-knacks. Cheetahs, elephants, giraffes, and tall women with svelte waistlines, gracefully adorned the aging carpet, silted fireplace, and chipping mantle piece. There was a huge square window in the center of the room with dingy heavy drapes that hang from it. The concentrated scent of collard greens and onions were forever embedded in them. Keenan could see a large tree with a tire that hung from a thick rope swinging in the yard. He could hear childish laughter muffled by the glass.

It smells like old people in here, he thought to himself as he turned to see the burly baritone standing before him. She wore a housecoat that gathered between her legs when she scooted her feet. Her hair collected in the front into a sculpted coiffure and was held together by passe' hair combs that had a few missing pearls. Her complexion was as dark as coal and her lips as thick as sorghum. Without moving them she spoke in a heavy creole accent, "Run, negriyon, run." Keenan was confused. "RUN, NEGRIYON, RUN!" She leaned in and screamed into his psyche.

Keenan jumped and Red squirmed to reposition herself on his chest. It was all a dream. He exhaled as he closed his eyes and savored the moment. She felt good...warm...soft. Creamy butterscotch freckles speckled her shoulders. He inhaled her natural earthy scent when she snuggled against her human pillow. Keenan boasted quietly to himself. *I could get use to this.* He wrapped his free arm around her, caressing her from her back to her waist. He feared the cadence of his heartbeat would awaken her. It pounded hard, threatening to break free from his ribcage. He wanted to touch it so bad. Red draped her thigh across Keenan's waist and suddenly her eyes popped open. She put her hands on Keenan's chest and quickly pushed herself away. "I'm sorry," Keenan pleaded abashed.

"Sorry about what?" Raysean rolled over sleepily.

Neither Red nor Keenan spoke. Red awkwardly glanced down at the king sized blanket. Raysean snatched the covers back to reveal a bulge in the tight work pants that Keenan borrowed from Gator. Raysean burst out in laughter. Keenan dived on his cousin to shut him up. He attempted to cover his mouth, but Raysean kept flopping around like a fish out of water. "I can't believe that you got...that you got...ahhhaaahahaaaha...you got a...ahhhaaahahaaaha..."

Raysean couldn't even get his words out for laughing so hard.

"Shut up! No, I didn't."

Keenan continued in his attempt to tie his cousin's lips into a knot - the kind of knot that you tie into a bread bag when you loose the twisty tie.

"Ok, dawg! Ok! Ok! Ok! I quit," Raysean said while trying to catch his breath.

Keenan was tall and muscular for his narrow frame. He was often mistaken for being a few years older. At just fourteen years old, he towered at five feet ten inches tall. Raysean trailed not far behind at five feet seven, except he was thicker in stature.

"I was sleep, dawg! That happens to er'nigga when he sleep, bruh. Quit playin! Plus, I gotta piss," Keenan said as he attempted to punch Raysean in the chest. Raysean blocked it and laughed, "Aight, dawg! I said – I quit! Fa real, dawg, I quit."

"It's too early to be up passing love licks, " Red drawled wiping her eyes and yawning.

Keenan stood and adjusted himself, "I really do gotta piss though," he said.

"Me too," Raysean interjected. Then, he jumped up and ran out of the room on his tippy toes to beat his cousin to it.

"Ahhh, this floor is cold," he screeched.

"That's what you get! You heard me say that I had to pee first!" Keenan yelled out with a Michael Jackson grip on his crotch.

The bathroom was directly adjacent to the den. Raysean applied pressure to the inside of his palms and set the mini corridor ablaze just as he had in the escape shaft.

111

Fresh lavender hung from the huge archway of the open privy. His toes cupped the grooves of the hand woven rug beneath his feet when he stepped inside. The rug was made from thin smoothed out branches held together by bright turquois twine and sealed by silky red tassels. It felt smooth and warm in contrast with the natural stone tile that encrusted the floor throughout the immaculate earthship.

In the corner of the room was an exquisite reclining soak tub carved from the pumpkin toned wall. It was more than three-feet deep and was elevated above three stoned steps that were accented by a lovely teal tile pattern.

On the other side of the steppingstones, was a large copper washbasin encased in a unique counter top that protruded from the wall. Identical tile covered its surface and separated the room. Connected by makeshift piping, was an even larger tub filled to its brim with water that sat inside of a clay base. Built in, was an adobe styled oven that housed hot coals burning aglow that kept the water steamy.

The toilet area wasn't as inviting, but was neither nearly as deterring as Raysean had originally feared. It was clearly there for functional purposes only. It was simply a shelf-like area sculpted from the wall with a wooden toilet seat attached. Raysean lifted the lid, and peered down the cold dark hole. A large white paint bucket aligned with a black garbage bag sat inside. A powdery green-like substance filled the bottom.

Good! No snakes.

He was also relieved that no unpleasant odors attacked him, as well. Raysean felt a sharp pain that coursed its way through his lower abdomen. He shifted from side to side in search of toilet paper.

No toilet paper? What the hell this girl be wiping with?

Raysean spotted a maple basket filled with folded rags fashioned from ripped towels and torn t-shirts beside the latrine. A covered wicker basket sat opposite side of him. He lifted the lid and saw a few soiled rags. Raysean returned the lid, wrinkled up his face, and plopped down on the toilet.

Must've been too much of that soup.

He began to sift through a tall stack of magazines that sat nearby. One after the other, they were generally all the same. Magazines on gardening, homesteading, and building natural habitats were stacked high and leaned like the Tower of Piza.

He selected the fourth one from the top. It had an eye-catching image of a little Himalayan girl that wore a beautiful magenta knitted cap with a bow on the side. In her petite hands overflowed juicy blackberries. A purple stain smeared her lips as she smiled with her bright asloped eyes. Her cheeks were a softly blushed rose.

His mind drifted off to Lotus. He wondered what she was doing at that exact moment. Was she all right? Did she know that he was coming for her? He imagined their reunion. He would scoop her up in his arms and kiss her right on her juicy fruits. And she would kiss him back, even more passionately than he had initiated. He would allow his hands to slide down her backside, but he wouldn't touch it, unless she arched it for him. Lotus wasn't *that* kind of girl, but she would be *his* girl regardless of what some dumb myth had to say about it. He knew he needed a plan. His thoughts shifted from fantasying to recollecting. In that intimate space, Raysean began to randomly recall the items from the chest that Ana opened before him. Images in his mind zipped by like a speeding carousel. Raysean was amazed that he could still, slow down, or speed it up at whim.

When he came upon a particular scroll in his mental catalog, he froze it to examine it more closely. It was the invisible door symbol. Below it was an inscription written in a calligraphy styled language. He identified its characters almost immediately. *Sanskrit.* He recalled it from one of the translation scrolls. His mind automatically interpreted the frail document from Sanskrit to Tibetan, and then from Tibetan to English.

Raysean began to read it aloud.

Unseeable Door Projection

Use with caution! MASTER SYMBOL FOR MASTER USE ONLY! Practitioners and apprentices - consequences for use is instant internal combustion.

Warning. Destination of door known only by the higher self. For use in dire purposes only. Once created, anyone can pass through. Use in conjuction with Omni-Closure Symbol Highly suggested. See Omni-Closure Symbol over→

Raysean flipped the ancient document over in his mental rolodex and located the Omni-Closure Symbol. He took another mental snapshot of it just to keep it fresh. Then he used his finger to air doodle The Unseeable Door Projection.

It glowed as it hovered in the atmosphere. Raysean blew onto it softly until it lay flush against the wall beside him. He cautiously stuck his hand through it to feel what was on the other side. Air. Open space. Raysean lowered his hand to floor level to ensure that there would be a ground this time. He was relieved to feel cool crunchy grass. His fingers followed veiny vines that sprawled up along a brick wall just before a voice fit for Heaven's choir startled him from inside of the other room causing him to snatch his arm back on to his side.

Red shook her head and giggled. "We need to get on up anyways. Help me fold this blanket up. Here, grab this end," she said.

Keenan backed up until his end stretched to its max. They both held the heavy blanket up high in preparation of the first fold. That's when Red began to hum. It was the same soulful hum that the old woman in his dreams hummed, except she started to sing the words as well. Red closed her eyes and belted out a long and emotional," *Lo-o-o-rd...*"

The chills went all over Keenan's body. She held that note like she was holding on to her own dear life. Red sounded as if she was channeling Mahalia Jackson from the other side. And just when she couldn't hold the note any longer, she softly cooed," *I'm not asking...for the riches...of this land.*"

"*L-O-R-D...*" Red called upon the almighty with the power to open up the heavenly gates, then she lightly uttered and projected the remaining verse of the southern hymnal from the pits of her soul, "*I'm not asking...for cathedrals...GREAT OR GRAND! But...what I'm asking you...Lord...is for a clean heart...and I'll...follow...theeeeeee...Give...me...a...cleeeeean...heaaaaart...and I'll...follooow...thee hee hee...*"

Keenan was mesmerized by the huge voice that flowed so effortlessly from someone so different than what he was used to.

115

"What are you staring at?" Red asked.

"My bad," Keenan responded, "but you – you just killed that shit."

"Keenan!" Red called out. She corrected Keenan's profanity by calling his name and elevating her voice.

"She was talking to me anyways," Raysean said from over Keenan's shoulder. His mouth was open from astonishment. Her ancestors seemed to rise up from somewhere from deep within and validated her dauntlessly.

"Dang, girl. Where you learn to sing like et?" Raysean asked.

"Thanks. This was our routine. Every morning, we'd get up when we were done sleeping. Muh'Dear always said that – that's when *spirit* wakes you up. She called it the *Witching Hours*. It's the time where we gave honor and respect to spirit and to our ancestors that walk in the light. You think I can sing? *Baaaby*, Muh'Dear could *saaang*! We would sing old songs as we made up our beds, then we'd burn sage and go to the big window to gaze at the moon until it disappeared into the light of day. That's how she knew all the juicy stuff about everybody that would come to get readings. The cards only tell you so much. At the end of the day, *you gotta be a clear channel*, Muh'Dear would always say."

"I thought that you said you wasn't no witch," Keenan antagonized.

"I ain't no witch. Witching Hours is just what they call it when you wake up between the hours of three and five in the morning. Muh'Dear said that it's the time when *spirit* finds it easier to come through. She said that they ride in on the mist of morning dew. Ain't no use in trying to stay sleep during the witching hours. Spirit won't let you. I usually can't lay back down until I do my morning rituals. That's why I don't even try to fight it."

Red turned to Gator who was still standing by the fireplace following her every word. "Gator, get my smudge bowl."

He already had it ready for her. Red lit the smoky wand in the fireplace and waved it through the air as she walked around.

"You know, there was a big window in my dream last night," Keenan revealed.

"Oooookay," Red over enunciated. She could *never* tell when he was being serious.

"You might wanna listen to him," Raysean said and then jokingly whispered, "he sees dead people." He clenched his lips tightly to fight off a laugh.

"Nuh uh," she rejected, "seriously?"

"On err'thang." Raysean put on his best serious face.

"Tell me more about your dream," Red eagerly said to Keenan.

"It was a big woman in my dream too," he smirked.

Red pranced over to Keenan and then punched him in the stomach.
"Muh'Dear...that's my baaaby. Don't play with my *baby*, lil boi."

Keenan laughed as he exaggerated his recovery from Red's powerless gut shot. "A baby can hit harder than et', but aight, I didn't mean it like et'."

He went on to describe the woman from his most recent dream to them, as well as, the big window that framed the big tree. Red was convinced that Keenan had dreamed of her old farmhouse.

"Did she speak? Did she say anything? Tell me what she said."

"Yea. She spoke in a weird language."

"What did she say?"

"She said," Run, negriyon, run!"

"Are you sure that's what she said?"

"Why? What does it mean?" Raysean asked.

"Run, little black boy, run," said Red.

"Run, little black boy, run?" Keenan asked. "Why would Muh'Dear tell me to run? Run where?"

"You asking me? She came to you, not me," Red sulked.

Red's eyes glossed, "Muh'Dear used to tell her clients, all the time, that once they got over their grief, they would get a visit from their loved one. But, I ain't seen Muh'Dear since Hurricane Katrina. And, who does she decide to visit this morning?"

Red rolled her eyes at Keenan. She had been waiting all of this time for Muh'Dear to come back to her just as all of her other ancestors had when she called upon them. But, it seemed that no matter how many candles she'd lit, Muh'Dear would never see her light.

"All of your dreams come true, huh? You a witch or something?" Red asked mocking Keenan.

118

Keenan raised his hands to his waist and smiled in a gesture of touché.

"Look man, you can be a witch. It don't even matter to me. I ain't crazy, neither. But, that don't keep the haters from calling me that. People call you witch. People call me crazy. Sooooo, whatever."

Raysean broke in, "Muh'Dear was warning us. I got a feeling that we need to get out of here fast. What's up with our clothes? Are they dry yet?"

Red nodded over her shoulder to Gator, "Go check on their clothes." Gator moved without hesitation.

Sensing Raysean's anxiety again, Red lightly gripped two of his short fat fingers with her dainty hand, and then grasped Keenan's long narrow ones in her other one. She tugged on them gently as she took a few steps backwards.

"Come on. Sit at the big window with me," she softly beckoned them. She lured them like bees on sweet honey. Red led them to the room that Keenan had followed Muh'Dear into in his dream, but it looked much different this time.

In the corner of the round room, were pillows – at least fifty assorted colors and sizes. She instructed them to grab three oversized pillows and to place them on the floor before the grand oval window. Red handed them each a single Dragon's Blood incense for protection and kept one for herself.

"What are we supposed to do with these?" Keenan asked.

"Light it from a candle and then stick it anywhere over there." Red pointed to hundreds of tiny holes in the clay wall.

119

Raysean followed Keenan over to the area where Gator was lighting the candles. He noticed that their clothes were neatly folded and stacked side by side on the floor against the wall. Their new Air Jordans were surprisingly as clean as they were when they first took them out of the box. They eagerly grabbed their belongings and awkwardly glanced over at Red who was attentively watching. She giggled," Ain't nobody looking at ya'll." Then she turned her head. Raysean and Keenan felt relieved to finally be wearing their own clothes again.

When the boys approached Gator, he turned around. The flame performed a graceful dance on the wick that protruded from the albescent stick of wax that the dead man held in his filthy cracking hand. He covered one side of the dancing flame with his other hand, bidding it still.

The cousins stuck their crumbly scented sticks into the fire. Each blew out their flame, leaving their tips smoldering and incandescent. They softly blew on their incense as they approached the dotted wall. Raysean and Keenan both slid their incense in the nearest holes in the wall and then sat down next to Red.

The blood moon no longer contained its tangerine glow. It was unclouded and illumined a satiny haze around them.

Keenan exhaled, "Wow. I don't think that I ever really looked at the moon before."

"Beautiful, right?" Red asked.

Raysean still felt anxious. "Shouldn't we be focusing on getting out of here?"

"And go where, Ray?" Red asked.

Raysean didn't have the answer, yet. Although he contemplated a few scenerios, none of them were foolproof. He knew that Grandmaw's house was out of the question if he wanted to keep them safe. As a loner, he never really had friends, nor never really felt the need for them. It was Keenan that was the social butterfly and considered his friends to be associates at best.

"Exactly," Red said. "This is why we need to sit. Trust me, the answer will come."

Her words confidently tumbled from her tongue, but inside she wasn't so sure. She sat before many moons awaiting a word from Muh'Dear, just like the others. They all came. Her mother, her aunts, and ancesters that felt familiar all showed, but Muh'Dear was still yet to be seen.

"Aight. We sitting. Now, what?" Raysean asked.

"Pick a spot on the moon...any spot...and stare at it. Your eyes will get blurry. You may even cry, but keep staring."

"This is stupid. We're wasting time."

"Go ahead. Be stubborn."

"I'm not being stubborn. I don't feel right about this."

"About what, Ray? You haven't even given it a chance."

Raysean didn't answer. He couldn't believe his eyes. Keenan's eyes...they were a lambent teal blue. They shifted as if he was watching someone or something. Then Raysean began to hear his thoughts, but they were vague. He was talking to someone. Raysean began to faintly hear the sound of another voice, except he couldn't make out the language. Whoever it was – was speaking in a language of high frequency tones that peaked at each pause. He knew that it was a language, because Keenan responded in English.

"Keenan!" Raysean called out to his cousin.

"Leave him alone!" Red interfered. "He's channeling. At least let me ground and protect him first."

Red rubbed her hands together, closed her eyes, and placed her hands on the soles of Keenan's feet. She imagined that he had roots growing from the bottom of his feet that bore deep into the earth's crust. Then she held her hands up and envisioned a halo of bright light surrounding him. Red began to speak," Keenan...I got you baby. Don't be afraid to channel. You're protected. Tell me, who's there with you?"

Keenan moaned, hesitated, and then spoke in a choppy accent," But, who else would it be, but me – the Nubian goddess herself, *Saaaaaaaada*," he hissed.

Red's voice trembled when she asked, "What do you want?"

"But, what else? To bring the masters home, young goddess. Ooooh, I know about you, *little girl*. It takes one to know one," Keenan earily snickered.

"Keenan, quit playing man!" Raysean screeched. He wanted so desperately for this to be one of Keenan's jokes, but sadly, he knew the truth.

"If you speak again and risk Keenan's safety, I will bind your mouth shut. Let me handle this," Red threatened Raysean. Inside, she knew that she would never make due on her threat, but she couldn't risk losing Keenan to the astral world. He could

122

end up a walking and talking zombie, like all of the deemed crazy people she carefully observed from a bird's eye view.

Raysean eyeballed Red. He knew instantly that her threat was empty, but he remained quiet, because there was something about Red that he instinctually trusted.

"Knock knock," Keenan spoke again.

"Who's there?" Red asked.

"Open the door...I'd hate to break a nail knocking it down."

Red safely broke the channel between Keenan and Saada by waving her hand in a chopping motion before the center of his forehead. In a flash, Keenan's eyes returned to their normal caramel color.

There was a loud knock at the door, followed by a loud explosion. The thick oak door imploded spitting splintered pieces throughout. Saada's stiletto boots clicked and made scuffing sounds against the natural stone flooring. There was a bright flash and smoke quickly began to fill the atmosphere. "Don't worry. It's just a little something to help you sleep. We have a long flight back to Africa...so chop chop."

"Gator," Red whispered.

Gator remained standing as he motioned for them all to get low. They did. He placed his hands across his lips, motioning them to be quiet as mice. Their hearts were racing a mile a minute. In the excruciating silence, Raysean recalled Muh'Dear's words to Keenan. His mind then shifted to the invisible door he'd practiced in the bathroom not long before. In an instant, he knew what to do. He didn't know where they'd end up, but at least it wouldn't be in a river again. He knew that for sure.

"There's no where to run," Keenan said in a panicked whisper.

"Sssssshhhh!" Raysean and Red hushed him.

"Come out. Come out, wherever you are. There's no where to run. Come on, now. This doesn't have to hurt. Although I am attempted to return the favor," Saada toyed while cat-like licking a wound on her arm, " I'll let your little girlfriend live, if you surrender without resistance."

Raysean locked eyes with Keenan. He began to speak telepathically to him.

"Cuz, when I tell you to run...run into the bathroom...we'll be right behind you...there's another door...an invisible one that I made when I used the bathroom...we'll be right behind you..."

"No, I ain't leaving you, dawg!" Keenan said aloud.

Red was amazed by their telepathic exchange, but this was no time for the wonder powers conversation she desired.

"You have a plan? What is it?!" She commanded.

"The bathroom...when I tell you to run...run! Keenan will go first...then you...then me...Gator doesn't breath, so these fumes can't hurt him. He will have to stay and protect us while we escape."

"No! Gator...he's coming with us!" Red insisted.

The crunching from Saada's heels piercing splintered wood neared. Raysean knew that this was no time to debate. "Aight,

124

Gator, you're coming with us...but only after we make it through the door first...if she comes after us...you better knock her head off..."

Gator looked to Red for approval. She nodded anxiously in agreement.

Raysean drew in a deep breath and slowly lip-synced his countdown," One...two...three...run!" He spoke in a harsh whisper.

Keenan wanted to move, but he couldn't. His hands and knees seemed to be glued to the floor.
"Run, nigga, run!" Raysean shouted.

Keenan took off like a bat out of hell, sliding across the hallway and into the bathroom like he was stealing home base. Red followed closely behind. A loud feline growl echoed throughout, bouncing off the walls as if in an amphitheater. They could hear the scratching of claws slipping against the floor's surface, as Saada gained her momentum. She was just a leap away from them.

Raysean dove into the bathroom in one just one spring and a roll, but not before Saada pawed his calf. Gator then tackled the big cat against the clay wall leaving a torso shaped indention in it. Saada roared and hissed as she fixed her eyes on Gator. The pain of inhaling his death permeated in her memory. It was foul and had her bedridden for an entire day. The tortuous nightmares that preceded his death now haunted her. Gator stood and cracked his own neck. Saada cautiously steadied herself.

Red's scream interrupted their stare down," Gator, come on!"

Keenan was already on the other side of the invisible door, leaving Raysean tugging on Red to go through next.

"Get off me! I'm not leaving without him. Gator! Do you hear me, boi? I said come on now!"

Raysean hated to do it, but it was the only thing to do. He grabbed Red by the back her shirt and slung her through the invisible door with all of his force. Then he eyeballed Gator, "You heard what the boss lady said. Let's go, man."

Gator kept his eyes locked on Saada as he scaled the wall and slipped backwards into the bathroom, just in time to see Raysean disappearing through the wall. Saada followed closely behind in a low crawl. She was sure that she had them right where she wanted them – in a corner. When Saada entered the bathroom, it was empty except for the overwhelming smell of decay that plagued her since her first encounter with Gator. *How was this possible, the walking dead*? She questioned all of her wisdom as she searched the room for their presence. She knew Raysean and Keenan's gifts through and through. *It had to be the work of the goddess child.*

Saada shifted and then paced around the room coveting Red's gifts.

I have to have them, she lusted.

Frigid rain droplets pelted down on them as Raysean scrambled to apply the Omni-Closure Symbol before Saada passed through the invisible door behind them. Once applied, he doubled checked the wall to see if it worked. The surface was hard and bricked again.

A strong herbal scent invaded their nostrils. Leaning against the wall smoking a blunt of cannabis was Hatin' Ass Jaquan. Raysean took one look at Jaquan, cracked his knuckles, and asked," Hatin' Ass Jaquan, what are you doing here?"

Jaquan glanced down at the herb and then back at them before responding, "Nah...what are you doing alive? This is your funeral!"

CHAPTER NINE

ASHES TO ASHES DUST TO DUST

"Liar!" Raysean shouted clenching his fists at his sides. He took a few steps forward and closed the distance between them.

Jaquan stiffened and braced for impact. This was it. The looming showdown between him and Raysean was finally about to take place – and in front of a girl. There seemed to be no way for him to weasel out of this one.

Jaquan cut his eye at Red and gulped.

"Hold on! Wait!" He attempted to proposition.

Raysean struck both of his extremities down with the force of lightening.

"Nigga, get your dick-beaters out of my face!"

"Hey!" Red interfered.

"This ain't got nothing to do with you, Red," Raysean riposted.

Jaquan winced in pain, cradling his burning hands. He was no fighter and wanted no parts of Raysean, that's for sure. He saw what he did to his sisters' father that day. It was a day that Jaquan would never forget. He was one of dozens that had front row seats in a crowd that had gathered to capture the drunken drama that had spilled out into Raysean's grandmother's front yard.

Jaquan captured the whole thing on his smartphone and instantly posted it to a popular social media site. The video of Raysean snapping that man's arm like a twig went viral before they boarded their school bus the next morning and so did the news that it was Jaquan that posted the video.

Raysean and Keenan approached him on the bus stop the following morning and confronted him about it. Keenan didn't say a word. He mainly just stood there like a referee about to give fighting rules for a title match. Jaquan had officially made Raysean's shit list.

"Did you post a video of the fight, my nigga?" Raysean inquired calm and daunting.

Jaquan responded like he felt any person in his shoes would respond. He lied. Aside from the reoccurring threats to stomp mud holes out of him, Jaquan actually considered Raysean to be a frenemy at worst and didn't understand why they couldn't *all just get along.*

The reasons Raysean had for wanting to bring harm to him were trivial in the least to Jaquan. He saw no harm in a little joke or two every now and then. People joked on him all of the time - like that one time on the school bus when Keenan waited until it was quiet as a church mouse to yell out a lethal one-liner.

"Jaquan, tell your shoes to shut up!"

Students on the bus squeaked and roared in laughter.

"That was a good one," Jaquan said with a satiric grin.

He wished that he'd thought of it first. He wished even more that his mother hadn't stolen the new shoes that his uncle bought him for the first day of school, leaving him no option, but to wear his old ones instead.

And then, it was that other time in class – the Monday after Thanksgiving break when Keenan waited on the opportune moment to yell out, "Jaquan, your family is so poor that ya'll had scratch and sniff turkey stickers for dinner!"

Jaquan had no comeback. Anything he said would be spun around and be used against him. Throwing jokes on Keenan's family was a setup, because it was the same as joking on Raysean's family – and Raysean just didn't play all of the time. It was situations like this that his gift came in handy. He used it to pick and chose his battles wisely.

He did this by identifying the gifts and flaws in other people. He was endowed with knowing a person's natural empowerment, yet in comparison with everyone else's talents, Jaquan often felt as if he had hardly any at all. He often coveted the gifts he easily recognized in others while secretly and sometimes openly criticizing those that were oblivious to their own.

"What do you mean this is our funeral?"

Keenan asked stepping in between the two to avert an inevitable head on collision. Although, the tension between Raysean and Jaquan had been brewing since the sixth grade, Keenan had no beef with him.

"It's been all over the news, man. Ya'll died," Jaquan panted with his arms outstretched to prevent any potential flying fists.

"Your grandmother thinks that ya'll missed your bus and must've went to Keenan's old foster mother's house to ask for a ride to school...then there was some kind of gas leak or something like that...that killed all three of ya'll. Word on the street...it was ashes to ashes...dust to dust, man."

"Stop lying! It's only been one day!" Raysean shouted pinning Jaquan to the wall.

"Get off me! It's been three days! It's been three days!" Jaquan shrieked.

He closed his eyes and put up the best and only fight of his life. With his fists clutched tightly, he swung about wildly in a windmill manner missing each and every time.

Red laughed aloud and motioned for Gator to break up the hilarious defense. Gator split the boys apart from each other with little effort. His might was so great that Raysean and Jaquan took flight before coming to awkward crash landings, opposite of the others'.

"Three days? What day is it?" Red asked.

"Thursday," Jaquan replied cautious of an impending pummel.

"That's not possible, is it?" Red asked. "Yesterday was only Tuesday."

Jaquan tossed his cellphone up to her, "Look, see?"

Red took it in her hands and marveled over it. She had never actually held one before. The only phone she'd ever used before was the lime green house phone that hung on the wall in their kitchen next to the pantry. She pitched the device back to him.

"It's so light."

"It hasn't even been released yet. My homeboy, Qaasim, gave it to me."

"We must've lost a day every time we went through those secret doors," Keenan chimed in.

Raysean's face skewed before he agreed, "Damn. Must have."

A young proper voice rounded the backside of the church interrupting them.

"What's taking you so long back there, Jaquan? It's about to begin."

Qaasim stopped in his tracks.

The steel grey Italian tailored suit he wore exalted his polished melanin rich skin. Yellowed scleras and burgundy brown irises peeked through tight eyelids. His lips were full and parted as his tongue rested between his teeth.

The soles of his Berluti loafers sank into the waterlogged soil. The Senator was going to be livid when he saw the sludge that encased his overpriced dress shoes, and he couldn't care less. He would just have to buy him more.

Qaasim was astounded by what he was witnessing.

"I knew it. You're still alive," Qaasim said with eyes ablazed with fervor.

His excitement dulled when he set his eyes on Red and her indentured slave. She rolled her eyes, in an exaggerated reflection of his noticeable disdain.

Qaasim extended a hand to his most trusted friend, Jaquan.

"Why are you sitting on the ground?"

"You act like we dawgs or something. We don't know you."

Raysean barked as he pushed Keenan's hand away when he tried to help him off the ground.

The rivals automatically checked their appearances. Raysean dusted off his Jordan sneakers and Jaquan lightly shook the slacks he borrowed from his rich friend.

Qaasim retorted with great admiration, "You're Raysean and you're Keenan. I'm Qaasim – a friend of a friend" he replied in a fading accent.

"Red cleared her throat, fluffed her hair and asked, "And, you knew this how?"

"The same way that I know that the man that stands at your side is not even alive. I can sense and manipulate frequencies. You seem to have an interesting encryption – a lock of sorts on yours, but the goddess code that you carry is unmistakable, queen," Qaasim admired as he inquisitively stepped closer to her.

He was enthralled by thousands of tiny streams of rainbow lights that parallelized and hovered just above the crown of her head. Qaasim squinted his eyes to see particles of light that squiggled and vibrated at different rates. A nigher inquiry revealed them to be numbers, billions of them. The young programmer gently strummed them with his fingertips. Red's body warmed when he cyber kissed her hand.

"Peace, queen. My name is Qaasim. A pleasure to meet you."

"You're so sweet," she blushed. The pleasure was all hers.

A woody fragrance with a hint of vanilla beans performed an aromatic dance for her senses. She inhaled him and exhaled a smile. Her cheeks flushed with cherry blossom and almond abstract splotches. His intoxicating pheromones were more than her boy crazy hormones could handle for the moment. Gator groaned and the cousins stepped up to her side.

"Queen?" Red blushed. "I don't look like a lil' ol' white girl to you?"

"Looks can be deceiving. It's frequencies that I trust," he said peering at Gator.

"Qaasim, son, the service is about to begin! Qaasim!" the Senator called out. Qaasim's visual query of Red was interrupted by the boisterous voice of Kentucky State Senator, Rich O'Conner.

"I'm coming!" Qaasim shouted. "I gotta go," he turned to the group and then continued, "I know the kinds of evils that pursue you, and it's imperative that you use this opportunity to get out of here before you're discovered. Some of the key players behind your attempted abductions will be sitting in the pews. But, that's just the tip of the iceberg. You'll want to get a good look at them. One in particular, is calling my name as we speak. Let's go, Jaquan. You know how paranoid he gets whenever you're around. Probably thinks we're back here getting high or something."

With bloodshot eyes, Jaquan responded with a Kanye shrug.

A warm gentle current blew through the crack of the stained glass window that the teens took turns peering through. They watched Grandmaw, their brothers & sisters, Raysean's mother and boyfriend, and their great-aunts take a seat on the front row before two copper urns with platinum trims.

A slideshow with images from the boys' lives flashed on a projector screen that hung above the choir. A Kirk Franklin song played somberly in the background. Poster boards with a collage of photos of Raysean and Keenan growing up were displayed on separate easels.

Family and friends, old and new, lined up one after the other to give hugs and say a few kind words to Grandmaw. She graciously accepted each condolence with a fragile smile. Her eyes were tired and weary. She hadn't slept since she went against her better judgment by allowing them to go off to school that morning.

Something told me that something wasn't right, she pondered as she fought to conceal her pain. *I should've never told them that I wouldn't take them to school if they missed their bus.*

A woman in the procession stooped down and whispered something in Grandmaw's ear. Grandmaw rubbed the woman's back and continued to sway like a pendulum. She didn't know how many more "they're in a better place" and "to be absent in the body is to be present with the Lord" statements she could take.

She didn't want them present with the Lord. She just wanted them home with her. *What did I do, Lord? Why do you keep taking my babies?*

Grandmaw's emotions welled high and threatened to flood a dam of mental agony.

Senator O'Conner, Qaasim, and Jaquan were the last in the procession to greet Grandmaw. Her skin crawled and stomach churned at first sight of them.

The lanky politician removed an envelope from inside of his dress coat, extended it, and leaned in for a few words.

Grandmaw lost it. The floodgates that held back a tidal wave of emotion, gave way. She yelped as if she'd seen a ghost. Aunt Sandy comforted her sister by pulling her close into her bosom. The Senator awkwardly glanced around to see who all had witnessed Grandmaw's reaction to him. He reluctantly noticed a detective that was videotaping with his smartphone from the end of the middle pew, as well as, a few reporters that he was familiar with.

Senator O'Conner then plastered a grin across his pasty face and passed the envelope to Aunt Sandy. She humbly accepted as her sister inconsolably wept. Grandmaw flinched when she felt someone caress the back of her luxurious hair.

"It's alright, mama," Raysean's father spoke.

Raysean lunged toward the crack in the window as if he could magically pass through it. Keenan covered his cousin's mouth to prevent him from drawing attention to them.

"Get off me! That's my daddy!" Raysean mumbled through Keenan's fingers.

"Ssssshhh! You want to *really* get us killed? You want to get innocent people killed? Whoever is after us got a whole lotta power, mane! I mean...they took out half the block coming after us! Like the African dude said, we need to figure out who the key players are," Keenan pleaded.

Raysean rolled his glossy red eyes, snatched away from him, and stomped away.

Red snickered.

"What's so funny?" Keenan asked.

Red shook her head in disapproval. "You said 'African dude' like you ain't African too," Red said and then went after Raysean. Gator followed closely behind.

Keenan sucked his teeth and gazed through the crack again. He searched for his uncle and found him and the prison escort seated on the other side of Grandmaw. She moaned and rocked from side to side as her only living child held her tightly in his arms.

The shackles that constrained his wrists were ironically the ties that bound them together again. She never wanted to let him to let her go. Seeing her son again, under those circumstances, was like taking the bitter with the sweet.

Raysean's father, Raymond, wore a blood orange jumpsuit, a well-maintained pair of white Nikes, and shackles on his wrists and ankles that linked by a heavy silver chain.

"Church say, amen," the rickety pastor commanded.

In a unified voice, the church said, "Amen."

"Church say, amen," the decrepit old man repeated as if he didn't hear them the first time.

"Amen," echoed the congregation.

The soundtrack faded out and the piano player began to play a peaceful piece that complimented the tempo and fluctuations of the pastor's grating utterances.

The only clear words that Keenan could make out were, "Let us pray."

In unison, church members and guests lowered their heads. The pastor prayed for what seemed to be an eternity. Some folks became restless and peeked around, while others – such as the Senator, went to sleep.

"I hate that disgusting pig," Qaasim whispered to his bestfriend. Jaquan leaned forward to get a good look at Qaasim's adopted father. His mouth was slightly ajar and revealed a set of yellowed lower incisors. He had an oblong nose with unkempt brownish red hairs that protruded from it. His skin was dry, thin, and transparent. His hair was slick, parted, and spiny. Jaquan shook his head, "He looks more like a possum to me." Qaasim sneered.

An older woman that sat behind them gave them a loud *sshhh.* Qaasim shifted uneasily in his seat. He had the utmost respect for his elders, but his adopted father was not a man. He was a monster.

"How bad could he be? You get anything that you want. You even got a black card."

"Yes, but at a price much greater than its reward. I hope that one day Allah will forgive me for the sins that I have committed for that swine. I would give it all away to find my family in Sudan. And, that day will come soon, with the help of your friends from public school. Inshallah."

"If my father was as rich as him – I wouldn't complain about nothing."

"Yes, well, there are just some things that are not for sale, my friend."

Qaasim held up a single protracted scrawny finger, flicked an area behind the Senator's head and then quickly drew it back down to his lap. Senator O'Conner's hair disheveled from flinching. His loud snort filled the entire room and beckoned every eye upon him. He awkwardly pulled out a finely embroidered handkerchief and wiped his flakey nose. Jaquan snickered, "What did you just do to him?"

"Remember that I told you that I couldn't hang out, because I was incredibly close to cracking a security code? Well, I did it. I cracked it. Nothing big really, but it's a start. If I'd known that I could hack people too, I would have disappeared a long time ago," Qaasim whispered.

Jaquan stared back at him blank faced.

"I hacked into his cerebellum for starters. It's the part of his brain that controls his balance. I just made him feel like he was free falling from a skyscraper," Qaasim japed.

Jaquan chortled, "You crazy, man. If he finds out that you hacked him..."

Sssshhh! The old woman demanded them mute again.

A visiting minister introduced the first solo singer.

Aunt Sandy removed her arm from around Grandmaw and stood onto her feet.

She was a slender woman with a combination of exotic and European features. A stunning violet dress sealed by a gold broach wrapped her like a present. Her smile was warm like homemade banana nut bread. Her teeth were as white as an ice-cold glass of milk. She sat down at the piano and adjusted the microphone.

"Praise the Lord, God's children. Weeping may endure for a night, but joy...joy cometh in the morning. He does not put more us than we can bear."

The church exploded with sporatic amens and hallelujahs.

Aunt Sandy tapped the foot pedal in between a dramatic crescendo. The self-taught piano player fingered the keys and rocked from side to side as a series of adlibs strung out from the pits of her soul. It could be heard in her voice, she was hurting. Her wordless utterances poured into the verbal amplifier as she held back an inundation of tears. She cued the choir by waving her opened palm in the air like a flag at half mass.

Just before her emotional dam broke, the choir coo'd in one harmonic voice.

I've gone

Through the fire

And I've been

Through the flood

I've been broken

Into pieces

Seen lightnin' flashin'

From above

But through it all

I remember

That He loves me

And He cares

And He'll never

Put more on me

Than I

Can bear

Aunt Sandy followed up with a bridge of raspy groans and melodic moans. A man stood onto his feet and yelled for her to take her time. Grandmaw stood up, waved her palms in the air, and cried, "You betta sing, Sandy!"

The choir repeated the chorus in unison.

"Scoot over," Raysean said as he returned from his emotional break.

"You alright, man?" Keenan asked.

"I'm cool. What's going on? Slide over. Let me see."

"Aunt Sandy is in there killin' it, dawg."

"Swear?"

Raysean's face lit up with excitement. They loved Aunt Sandy. She was their favorite aunt. When they were younger, and had sleepovers at her house, she would allow them to be "king for a day." They loved it, because they could eat cereal at night and pizza in the mornings. She also had cable television with every station and flat screen televisions in every room. She was a traveling nurse practitioner for a living and put her career on hold to care for her niece, Keenan's mother, in her last days. The boys' cheeks mashed together when they each peered through the broken stained glass window to catch a glimpse of her. She led the choir by emotionally singing the beginning of each line of the chorus.

Grandmaw sobbed aloud. Her grief spread like wildfire in that place and her cathartic embers seemed to catch on to every other person in the sanctuary. The whole place wept, even the prison guard that escorted Raysean's father for the day.

Raysean and Keenan heard sniffling from behind them. Red was crying a river.

"Whatchu crying for?" Keenan inquired.

Red wiped her eyes against Gator's sleeve, "It's just so sad."

"What's so sad? We're right here in front of you," Raysean snickered.

"Why do you always have to act so hard? All of it. Do you even get that you're dead to them? This is it. You'll never be a family again," she snapped.

Raysean and Keenan were momentarily at a loss for words. It hadn't hit them yet. They were dead. Dead to the world.

"Me and Gator er' dead to peoples back home too. And if you don't know what that means...it means you on your own...and it ain't easy, baby...it ain't easy."

"We can fix this now. All we have to do is walk in there and let them see us," Raysean resisted.

"We can't," Keenan retorted. "I just heard your dad's thoughts. Grandmaw doesn't know it yet, but he is going to be released early next week on a pardon. If we walk into that church, we might mess that up. Grandmaw needs him. Our sisters and brothers need him, dawg. I'm not saying that we'll never be back but...we..."

Raysean let out a puff of air, blocked Keenan out, and peered through the crack again. He hated not being in control. He hated not knowing what to do.

"Aw, *hell* naw. What the hell is he doing?" Raysean said.

"Who?" asked Keenan.

"Hatin Ass Jaquan. He's on the mic."

The side of Keenan's face squished against Raysean's when he peeked through.

Jaquan tapped the mic, blew in it, and chuckled.

"Can ya'll hear me? Me, Keenan, and Raysean...we go back. We go back like scratch and sniff turkey stickers."

The congregation murmured and laughed softly.

"Nah, fa' real though," Jaquan glanced at the sky, "Keenan...I'ma miss your jokes and Raysean...uhh...I'ma miss your *friendship*...and if I could ask God for a favor...it would be to play one last game of twenty-one with ya'll at Russell Lee Park."

"We ain't never shot no ball with that jerk," Raysean said.

"Sshh. I'm in his head. It's where him and Qaasim want to meet up after the funeral," Keenan replied.

"When, after the funeral?"

"Hold on. I'm asking him now."

Jaquan ended his last words by saying, "one last game...*after* I eat some of that good chicken that I smell downstairs...that chicken smells *good*."

"Tell that fool that we got his message...and get off the mic before we haunt his ass...we'll catch up with them in a couple hours."

Detective Nunnely stood on the curb as he assisted Grandmaw into the limo. Grandmaw held his hand tightly when he tried to pull away.

"Something ain't right, detective. First that young girl, Lotus, now my grandsons? I got a feeling that my grandsons are dead, because of what they saw," Grandmaw said as she searched his face for understanding.

141

"Promise me that you will look into this," she pleaded with hollow eyes.

"I will do everything that I can, Ms. Lewis." Detective Nunnely closed her door and rubbed his fingers as he watched the car pull off. Her firm grasp left them pasty and webbed.

When the detective looked up, he saw an all black Camaro slowly following the Senator's SUV a few cars back. The back passenger side window was lowered revealing only the eyes of a woman staring at him intensely. He pulled out his cell phone, took another look at the image that Raysean had drawn during his interrogation, and glanced back up at her. She and the woman in the image were identical.

Detective Nunnely eyed the license plate as it crept by. A perfect match.

"Stop! Hey...stop!" he shouted waving his hand.

The maroon woman mouthed something that he couldn't make out. Her window crept up and the car revved its engine as it peeled out barely whipping around Senator O'Conner's Cadillac Escalade.

The Camaro's back wheels extended out revealing two more doors as it drifted around the stop sign.

Well, I'll be damned. All black err'thang fo' do' Camaro," the detective sighed.

CHAPTER TEN

SAADA

Saada gazed into the mirror in search of herself. She was
beginning to no longer recognize the woman staring back at her
and the dreadful things that she had done in the name of righting
her wrongs had her enslaved to her evening's reflection.

She pulled her long locks back and wound them up around her
head forming a beauteous crown. Saada then dropped her posh
robe to the floor and admired her naked body. It had a natural
sable polish beneath the elegant vanity lights.

Her glance fell upon the hideous scar that lined her jawline just
under her ear and her admiration quickly faded. An inch closer
and Saada would be down to eight lives - one less than the nine
she was born with. And to Saada, that was not a lot, considering
that her adversary was an immortal.

Saada briefly recalled the moment that Ana unleashed the
shurikens that nearly sliced her jugular. She winced,
remembering the pain, not from the gash, but from finding them
together. Saada discovered Ana and her lover, Lucus, lip-locked
in a tight embrace. He was supposed to be there to break it off
with her – ending things before it could develop into anything
serious, but instead they stood before Saada kissing.

She didn't recall all of the details. Saada just remembered that
when she lunged at Ana, Lucus stepped in between them. This
allowed Ana the opportunity to release a series of silver
shurikens from a place hidden within her leather wrist wraps.
The razor sharp tip of one of the tiny throwing stars nipped the
side of Saada's face. Warm scarlet blood spray freckled Lucus'
cheek. Saada felt her gaping wound. Her fingers were coated in
blood.

The room seemed to shrink and the floor felt as if it was
trembling. Saada blacked out, and for the first time ever, she
involuntarily shifted from pure rage. When Lucus was finally

able to intervene, Ana lay twisted and crumpled, encircled by massive bloody paw prints.

She reminisced watching Ana's eyes glaze over when she killed her the first time.

If only her death were permanent.

Being that she had the gift of resurgence, Saada knew that it was only a matter of time before they would meet face to face again.

And, when she arises from the ashes, I'll be ready.

Saada stepped into the marble steam shower to cleanse herself in preparation to make salaat. She silently declared her intention for worship.

Allahu Akbar, from all of my blessings flow.

As the steamy mist fell on and all around her, she closed her eyes and began to slowly suck her fingertips, lick the backs of her hands, and the inside of her wrists. She purred like a kitten nestled against its mother's fur. Her eyes and neck rolled seductively as she softly caressed her face and body in intervals. She sat on a ritzy bench that protruded from the wall and displayed her master yogi flexibility when she tucked her leg behind her head. Saada resembled a seated ballerina with her foot arched and her toes begging to dance on the ceiling.

Saada continued her cleansing as she passionately licked the inside of her thigh, her firm round buttocks, and proceeded to cleanse her yoni when her phone began to ring.

She sprung up and fetched it from the charger. It was her comrade, Nadia.

"As Salaam Alaikum, sister. Please tell me that you have good news."

"Wa Alaikum Salaam, Saada. I was able to locate the records that you requested on all of the children from The School of Understanding Self in the last fifteen years. Out of four thousand three hundred and ten children, eighty of them were of African decent. Of those eighty, thirty-five of them were boys and out of that pot leaves one boy fifteen years of age, adopted by Senator Rich O'Connor. I'd say that's some pretty darned good news."

Saada's emotions felt like they were on a trampoline.

Could it really be him?

She wondered if it truly was the son that Ana stole and sold into adoption from The School of US.

"Saada? Are you still there?"

"Ah, yes. I'm here," she stuttered and continued in a more confident tone.

"What does he look like? Do you think that it's really him this time?"

"According to Kuten Qi, he would be found in the custody of the United States government. She's never been wrong. You know that. I just uploaded everything, including a picture. You should have a look for yourself."

Saada took a fluffy white towel from a floating glass shelf on the wall and wiped the foggy mirror clear. She then accessed the file that Nadia sent from a high tech computer hidden inside of the looking glass and expanded the image.

A smiled parted her lips.

"He has my eyes."

"Indeed," Nadia chimed in. "Indeed."

Senator O'Connor suspired and answered his phone on the first ring.

"Senator O'Conner?"

"Who is this and how did you get access to this line?"

"My name is Saada and I believe that you have something that belongs to me."

"I know who you are. And, as I recall it, you abandoned your baby boy."

"If you knew who I was, then you'd speak to me with a much higher regard!"

She was right. Saada's reputation was well renowned amongst secret societies for being a black cat that you never wanted to cross your path. He knew that he had just been threatened. The Senator wore a vexed grimace when he glanced over at Qaasim and Jaquan.

He didn't want to have this conversation in front of them. The last thing he needed was the world's greatest programmer to discover that his mother was alive and then go rogue on his watch.

Qaasim and Jaquan appeared to be engaged in a flurry of whispers.

Senator O'Connor cupped one hand around the receiver and stood his ground.

"You are also in possession of individuals of great interest to me."

Saada purred a long egregious chortle, "I see. That was your plan all along, an exchange. Well, you see, The Original Gods don't negotiate. That method perpetuates genocide and oppression of our people. We prefer to annihilate our threats, instead."

"Who are you kidding? You haven't been in contact with a member of The Original Gods in more than a decade. You abandoned ship, remember? And, since you went AWOL, your entire organization has dismantled. There are no more Original Gods – except for maybe an overzealous girl with a broken heart."

The Senator's words cut deep and stole her breath for a moment. *That traitor Ana left out no details, did she?*

He was right. Saada abandoned her allies, along with a loyalty covenant sworn never to be broken. She knew that she could not go up against a world super power alone and that she would need to make things right if she was going to call her old squad for assistance.

Saada went for the verbal kill.

A verocious lie growled from her lips, "Kuten Qi prophesized your death by my jaws tonight. And, I'm going to chew you up and spit you out."

"That's impossible. It was written before my birth that I would be president."

"Must I remind you that her accuracy is one hundred percent?" Saada retorted.

Senator O'Conner nervously tapped end on his touchscreen. He confirmed that the line was dead before making a much-dreaded phone call.

A man with a deep voice answered in an unperceivable tongue that bubbled and gurgled as if he was speaking under water, "It appears that your side dealings have gotten you caught in your own snare. Now, you have a rogue Original God on your hands that just happens to be the best tracker that The School of US has ever trained!"

"I have a plan…"

"Silence, you half-breed imbecile!"

A sharp pain coursed through the Senator's head.

He gripped both sides of it in agony.

"I think something's wrong with the Senator," Jaquan said nudging Qaasim.

Qaasim looked over at his adoptive father and observed what resembled static electricity inside of a particular group of multicolored light streams that towered above his head and replied, "I think someone's trying to read his mind."

"So, that was your plan in adopting the boy? But, how did you know that Lotus and Kuten Qi would be kidnapped by The Original Gods a decade before it happened?"

The voice from the phone interrogated him while violently sifting through his conscience and caused him to drop his phone from psychological torment.

As the pain subsided, Senator O'Connor flashed the boys a phony smile in effort to assure them that there was no need to be alarmed.

He then retrieved his cell phone from the floorboard of the SUV. Cherry-red spots speckled his handkerchief when he dabbed his nostrils. His hand trembled as he slowly raised the phone back up to his ear.

The voice began to gurgle again.

"Your presence is required in Washington, D.C. tonight. Bring the boy!"

The Senator's voice wavered and cracked.

"Yes, sir, Mr. President. Yes, sir."

Saada's entire body trembled with dread as she made an international call.

A man with a sensual tone and alluring accent answered.

"Hello?"

Saada closed her eyes, momentarily savoring his voice.

"Hello? Saada, is this you?"

Saada gasped and a single tear trailed into her hair when she tilted her head back. She wanted to speak so badly, but she feared she would actually do it - ask him for his help. Although she knew that he would do anything for her, her pride was too great for that. This may have been their issue, but it was her problem to fix. She was the one that gave their child up out of spite, only to have him sold in adoption by a scorned lover.

Saada's fingernails, lustre-black and carved into sharp points, hovered above the hang up icon on the touchscreen. She thought that she was ready to have *the conversation*, but her doubts quickly set in the moment that she heard his voice.

A handsome Jamaican patois hid behind his bouncy Brixton, London idiom.

"Please don't hang up. I know it's you. The cadency of your breath gives you away every time. It reminds me of a time when...I didn't mean to hurt you, Saada."

She parted her lips, but her words were blocked by a lump in her throat.

"These calls are getting further apart and fewer between. Say something. Anything. Say you hate me! Just go ahead and say it! Say something. I just need to hear your voice," Lucas pleaded passionately.

Saada noticed a dark apparition billowing from the shadow of her phone on the floorboard. She nervously yanked the drawstring on the shade above the windows and killed the sunlight and her shadow along with it, ruining Lucas's attempt at an umbrageous teleport.

"Why do you keep shutting me out, Saada? It's been fifteen years."

You know why!

Saada pressed the end icon so hard that it cracked the screen. She threw the device out of the window, dabbed the corner of her eye, and spoke aloud to her loyal friend, "Nadia, switch to stealth mode. Put us in the air just below the radars. Destination...Senator O'Connor's house."

The shadow from the smashed smart phone cast itself onto the pavement, eclipsed into the pole of the traffic light, and automatically blended in with the shadow of the sports car that was Nadia's temporary body.

"Nadia, set us down right behind those trees over there," Saada said.

She hovered and landed behind a dense layer of woods without making a sound.

Nadia was Saada's right hand man and a master of possessive teleportation. At her whim, she could possess and manipulate the body of inanimate objects and sentient beings.

Her insatiable lust for vanity aroused a preference in beautiful, wealthy women with expensive tastes for vehicles that were fast and furious. Like an artist with an eclectic eye, she often put her own spin on the body once she attained it – which she could easily possess with simple eye or physical contact.

When she would possess a body, she would often taper the side of her hair, as a declaration of her underlying true self. If it was a vehicle, she loved to customize it with stealth and flying abilities. But, no matter whom or what Nadia took possession of, she vowed to never become them. She still had hopes of reclaiming her real body, which was lying in a coma-induced-state inside of an arcanum hospital on the island of Madagascar.

Saada decided to visit Nadia on the day that she went underground. She held Nadia's hand and vented her heartache. Saada promised to return only after she found her son and made things right. As she said her emotional goodbyes to her dearest friend, Nadia used part of her remaining life force to possess Saada before she could turn to walk away.

Saada felt as if she was a passenger in her own body. She helplessly watched Nadia grab a pair of shears from a table and stand before a mirror above the sink. Nadia scooped up a lock of Saada's dreads in one hand. The mouth of the scissors were open and hungry in the other. She always tried to convince Saada that she was a Mohawk girl.

Nadia smiled at Saada's reflection and placed the shears back down on the sink.

"Just kidding. You'd kill me if I cut your hair," she humored.

A nurse walked into the room to check the vitals of Nadia's helpless body. Taking a bullet in the head for her twin brother, Lucus, during the student rebellion was a selfless act. She stood beside the nurse to take a look at herself. Her head was wrapped in a bandage and her eyes were bruised and swollen shut. Nadia's body seemed to have tubes and wires attached to every inch of it. A machine alongside of the bed breathed for her.

Nadia's tears fell from Saada's eyes. This was a goodbye *for now* for her, as well.

The nurse handed her some tissues, "I can see that you were close," she consoled.

"More than you will ever know," Nadia said before turning and walking out.

Nadia spotted a brand new Porshe parked in valet when she sashayed out of the automatic doors of the secret medical facility. It felt so good to finally be free from that bed. Her fingertips slid from the hood of the luxury vehicle to its driver side door, simultaneously unlocking them.

Saada found herself back in control of her body and standing outside of the running vehicle. She was slightly confused.

Nadia's voice blared through the speakers, "Hop in! Surely, you didn't think I'd let you go alone. After all, he is my nephew."

Saada attempted to get into the driver's seat and Nadia slammed her doors shut.

"Have I really been asleep so long that you've forgotten the proper etiquettes of riding in me? Number one, don't touch the radio. And number two, take a back seat."

Climbing inside of the back of Nadia's passenger side, Saada shook her head and evinced a smile, "Let's get the hell out of here."

"Keep her running. This shouldn't take long. If I'm not back in twenty minutes, come and get me." Saada said.

"Twenty minutes on the clock," Nadia's sultry voice boomed through the speakers of the Camaro.

Saada stepped one foot out of the car revealing a crocodile thigh-high boot with a black tourmaline stiletto. Her second foot shifted into a shiny hind leg before it touched the cold crunchy earth. The rest of her body pounced out of Nadia's temporary avatar on all fours.

Saada sprinted at top speed until she reached the back of the Senator's mansion. She transformed back into her body and walked stark naked into Senator O'Connor's six-car garage. There was a Corvette, two Hummers, and two Mercedes. Saada flattened the front tires of each vehicle with the tips of her nails as she flounced by them. Before walking into the house, she spoke aloud," Kill the lights and override the security system."

The entire house went black.

"Lights dead," Nadia replied through a micro ear bud embedded in Saada's inner ear.

"Thanks."

"You have movement in the kitchen, exactly four feet from the garage door."

"I already picked up their scent. I'm guessing – a man and a woman by their pheromones. This should be interesting," Saada replied.

She smirked and stepped cautiously inside.

"There's been a change of plans. Son, I'm afraid that you're going to have to settle the score on the court with Jaquan another time. We have an unexpected trip to D.C. tonight. Driver, reroute to Victory Park, instead. We're taking Jaquan home."

Qaasim and Jaquan side-eyed each other.

"What about meeting up with Raysean and Keenan?" Jaquan whispered to Qaasim.

"And, Red," Qaasim added with a gleam in his eye.

"Aw, man. Somebody's crushing hard on the big booty white girl."

The friends snickered obstreperously and the Senator shook his head.

Why his adopted son insisted on having such an *ignorant* friend was completely beyond his comprehension.

Senator O'Conner briefly recalled the day that Qaasim chose Jaquan. It was the day that the Senator went to speak at a press conference for the re-opening of the Parkland Boys & Girls Club in the West End of Louisville.

He had tried on many occasions, to no avail, to socialize Qaasim with the children of his constituents and the more affluent. In the Senator's world, it was just "us" and "them".

Why, on earth, would anyone want to be associated with them? Qaasim was just used to a more diverse group of friends at The School of US. And, regardless of what region of the world they came from, it was the Africa inside each of them that he resonated with.

They all came from modest backgrounds. His friends from school were; Nahjah from India; a powerful cultivator; Alex from Brazil, a life graffiti artist; Carlos from Cuba, a high-tech mechanical engineer; Rocko from Oakland, an anarchist illusionist; and Sahai from Jamaica, a futuristic inventor. And, although they all secretly stayed in contact with each other, they were still oceans and mountains away.

"Him. I want him," the wealthy politician recalled five-year-old Qaasim say as he tugged on his coattail.

"What?" Senator O'Conner asked behind a well-rehearsed smile.

"You said that if I cooperate, I could have anything. Well, I want a *real* friend and I want him."

Senator O'Connor turned his nose up at a younger Jaquan standing in the center of a group of older boys pointing and laughing at them. He stood shirtless in an oversized pair of sagging jean shorts and a pair of worn Air Jordan sneakers. Broken glass and paraphernalia outlined his feet like chalk lines at a murder scene. A urine-scented breeze gently ushered an empty potato chip bag by them like tumbleweed in the desert.

"Him? Why him? Why don't you want to associate with your own kind?"

"He is my own kind," a young Qaasim pouted, a preview to a full-blown tantrum.

"Okay. Okay. You can have him, just as long as you start cooperating, agreed?"

"Agreed."

Qaasim had already ruined a classified trip to Alaska when he shut down the entire network after discovering the truth about the intentions of the program that he had written for it. He had been adamant about going back "home" ever since. Senator O'Connor tried to shower him with any and everything that he thought would make a child with his talents happy.

Within the week of Qaasim's arrival at Victor Sire Estates, the Senator had already spent over a half of a million dollars on computer equipment alone, making Qaasim's bedroom an exact replica of the state of the art lab that he enjoyed so much at The School of US.

But, it was still not enough. Qaasim was homesick.

Victor Sire Estates was a handsome horse ranch that sprawled out on nearly fifteen hundred acres of rich Kentucky Bluegrass. Boasting with countless *awe* factors, Victor Sire Estates' most fond features were its six monolithic barns that sat on endless manicured lawns that rolled and bantered.

Senator O'Connor recollected Qaasim's innocent eyes sucking in all of the grandeur like a cool swirly straw. His mind flooded with dreams of grooming and riding those big shiny horses.

It took Qaasim less than a week to realize that he had been bamboozled. He was not gaining a kind and wealthy American father – the kind he'd seen on his favorite television show, but instead, a powerful and gluttonous pawn in a deadly game.

He soon discovered that the adopted life wasn't the fairytale that The School of Understanding Self carefully cultivated into his mind and the minds of others also void of their mother and father.

Instead, it was more about greed and deception – money and power.

"Red *is* a very attractive young lady and I think that the feeling is mutual."

"What do you think that zombie thinks? He ain't gonna let you no where near her." Jaquan joked.

"I think that he takes his orders from her. It's Keenan that I expect to feel some kind of way. It's obvious that he's hot for her. But, what we really need to figure out is how to ditch the Senator so that we can meet up with them," Qaasim whispered.

"I have an idea."

"What do you have in mind?" Qaasim asked.

"I gotta give you this suit back, right? Well, we just gon' walk through the front door and run straight out the back."

"Yea, sure. But, what about your auntie? She might ask questions," Qaasim doubted.

"Questions about what, mane? She don't care about me, dawg. I'm grown."

"She's the least of all of our worries. When an asset runs, the protocol is to send a tracker and to dispatch drones. Cameras will be our first downfall and they're everywhere – on nearly every traffic light and light pole, as well as, on just about every cellular phone. If face recognition zeroes in on us, we're screwed. I know. I designed it. You say you know the West End like the back of your hand, well, now is the time to show and prove. So, I'll ask you again. What do you have in mind?" Qaasim whispered.

"Remember the girl that I told you about that sits in front of me in homeroom?"

"Yea, Ashley, the girl that you crack jokes on all of the time. She can make herself invisible. What about her?"

"Well, she lives right behind my house."

"And? What does she have to do with anything?"

"It's kinda like this…we have an arrangement worked out. Raysean was on some other shit as usual, so I approached her with a deal. I told her that I would chill with the jokes, if she would make me invisible whenever I asked her to. I knew that she could do it, because she would make her dog invisible when she walked him around the block. To keep it all of the way real, I was really gonna catch the dope boys high and slipping, feel me? But, we could use her to get us to the basketball court without being noticed."

"Honk the horn," Senator O'Conner ordered the driver.

The driver blew the horn of the blacked out luxury SUV.

Someone yelled, "Five O," and the crap game in Victory Park dispersed like cockroaches when the kitchen light comes on.

"Great! They think that we're the po po's," Senator O'Conner huffed.

God damn it, Qaasim. What's taking you so long?

Senator O'Connor told the driver to go and knock on Jaquan's door. A woman in her late twenties wearing a black silk scarf wrapped around her head, a University of Louisville t-shirt, and a pair of black leggings opened the screen door before he could knock.

"You got a warrant, officer?" she asked filming him with her cellphone in one hand.

"Uh hello, ma'am. I'm not the police. I'm Qaasim's driver. Could you please let him know that his father is getting a little anxious? He told me to tell Jaquan not to worry about the suit. Consider the Armani suit to be a gift from the Senator."

The woman sucked her teeth and advised," They gone."

"I'm sorry?"

"I said…they gone…out the back door…about ten minutes ago."

"Ten minutes ago? We drove up ten minutes ago. Where did they go?"

"I don't know."

"What do you mean, you don't know? You don't keep tabs on your kids?"

"First of all, you can get the fuck off my porch with all of that bullshit. You don't know me! You don't know all I gotta deal with downtown behind that lil' muthafucka...got me missing work and shit! You gon' pay my rent if they try to put me out? You gon' turn my lights back on when the people come out and cut my shit off? If I put my hands on him, then ya'll be tryna charge me. Plus, while you meddling – I ain't his mammy. I'm his auntie. I got my own damn kids to worry about..."

The woman continued to vex her frustrations as the driver skipped down the cracked steps, around the front of the vehicle, and hopped in.

"They're gone!"

"What? What do you mean they're gone?"

"Gone where?"

"Jaquan's aunt didn't know. Apparently, he does this often."

"This is not happening!" Senator O'Conner screamed punching the driver's seat.

He buried his face in his hands. Two flushed fist prints remained when he removed them.

He retrieved a burner phone from his inner jacket pocket and dialed dispatch.

"Send me the best tracker that you have and some muscle! The asset has run."

"We know. We were still listening in even after you hung up with Saada. Must I remind you that the *best* is already in pursuit of you? Dispatching drones and activating worldwide face recognition as we speak. It shouldn't be long before Big Brother picks him up," the agent replied.

"Which unit are you sending?"

"Not a unit. A child."

"A child?"

"She's no ordinary child. Her hunting skills are subpar to none and she's getting keener each day. And, I must warn you against her appearance. She may look like an innocent twelve-year-old girl, but beyond those angelic eyes wields the power to summon and command spirits and principalities. So, if I were you, I'd stay on her good side. Her estimated time of arrival is now."

In an instant, a gush of wind filled the SUV. Everything not snapped on or glued in got caught up in a miniature twister. Senator O'Conner turned when he heard and felt a thud from behind him. There sitting with her head down was a child wearing a wool, hooded cape that covered her body and filled the backseat entirely.

The Senator gulped and greeted her, "Hello."

"Hi," she softly returned his salutation from beneath the heavy cloak.

The Senator slowly removed her hood. He was amazed to see dozens of tiny braids that swirled and crossed each other, creating the glorious Flower of Life mandala at the crown of her head. Two sideburn braids with hundreds of citrine crystals strung on them, hung long and disappeared beneath the weighted cloth. She had the complexion of bronze and the eyes of flames.

"My name is Senator O'Conner. What's your name?" He asked politely.

"Seraphima," she susurrated.

Raysean stood up and walked a few paces down the ramp of the viaduct behind John F. Kennedy Elementary School.

"Where you going?" Keenan asked.

"Man, I don't feel right. It's like somebody's watching us," Raysean scoped around.

"You just paranoid. Nobody, but Grandmaw would look for us here...and why would she...when she thinks we dead?"

"Ain't nobody noid', man. Red, remember how you said that you could feel us like you could feel your own skin? It's just like that. What do you feel?"

"I feel the same way…like there are others like us close by. Maybe it's Qaasim and Jaquan. I'll check and see."

Red glanced around until she located a small group of birds devouring fried chicken wing scraps. A hot sauce stained food boat lay upside down nearby. Stale french fry crumbs were scattered around it. She closed her eyes and whistled a hypnotic birdcall. The birds simultaneously flew off with a sense of urgency.

"I put my eyes in the sky again to see if they are at the court yet. I think I see them. Yea, it's them." She said.

"You sure?" Keenan asked.

"Of course, I'm sure. I have thirteen birds in the air, each with their own view. I see the boys running the back way, through the woods. They look scared."

"They probably hot and leading the heat straight to us." Raysean sulked.

"Do you see anybody chasing them?" Keenan inquired.

"Naw, and they ain't running no more either. They peeking through the trees, more than likely looking for us. Good thing, I told Gator to hide there. They don't see him, but he's crouching right behind them," said Red.

"I don't see it! Where did it go?" Qaasim panted in a full panic.

"I don't know, but it got Ashley. I saw it swoop that big girl up like it was nothing and drop her!"

"What was that thing and how could it see us? Did you see how many wings it had?"

Jaquan parted his lips to respond, but a pale grimy hand smothered his words. Gator held his other hand outstretched and beckoned Qaasim to remain quiet. Qaasim signaled to Jaquan to halt his stifled screams, useless kicks, and pelts.

161

Gator then lowered Jaquan back to the ground and removed his hand.

He placed one finger on his lips and motioned them to be quiet. Then he pointed through the trees at police sealing off the area. A helicopter buzzed above them. With a nod, Gator gestured for them to follow him. He safely led them to the underpass where the others anxiously awaited.

"Something's after us! We gotta get out of here!" Qaasim cried affright.

"Something's after you! We got our own problems! Let's go, man! They brought the heat right to us." Raysean scurried about.

Suddenly, the underpass filled with the sound of swift beating base drums. They were all jolted at what they were witnessing. Seraphima hovered in midair before them. She had six translucent wings – two covered her eyes, two covered her feet and two she flew with. Her eyes burned with enough passion to consume an army.

"What the fuck is that?" Keenan exclaimed.

"Some kind of human angel or something," Jaquan said.

"She's part seraphim," Red added.

"Isaiah 6: 2 - Above him were seraphim, each with six wings: With two wings they covered their faces, with two they covered their feet, and with two they were flying. You might be right. I remember reading about them in the bible, as punishment, when I was younger," Raysean input.

"Muh'Dear used to tell me about them all of the time. They are my favorite type of angel, because they sit the closest to God," Red said.

"Are all angels good guys, because I saw that thing pick Big Ashley up and drop her on her ass?" Jaquan debated.

"Cuz, you might want to get one of those invisible doors ready, just in case." Keenan said.

Raysean turned and drew the first tier in the air. Then, Seraphima swooped down and scattered them all in different directions from the mighty force of her wings. Gator was the first back onto his feet. He ran as fast as he could and leaped onto Seraphima's back. She shook him off by flapping her wings. Then she flew down and pinned him down in a full mount. Seraphima uncovered her face. Gator cowered in fright. She drew a massive energetic saber from an invisible sheath on her back and held it to Gator's throat. Her two waist length braids fell against his face. The citrine stones that encased them burned his cheek. They each contained the power of the sun. The side of Gator's hair engulfed up in flames from merely brushing against them. He patted his head wildly and groaned in agony.

Red commanded a flock of birds to attack. They each attempted to maraud Seraphima with their sharp beaks, but fell dead at her feet when she uncovered her face again.

"Ya'll see that? She killed those birds by just looking at them!" Keenan screamed.

"Whatever you do...don't look at her face!" Raysean asserted.

"How in the hell do we fight this thing?" Jaquan asked.

"It's me that it wants," said Qaasim stepping out into the open. Seraphima flew into the air. She opened all of her wings and then dove towards him.

"Shield!" Red exclaimed.

And, a shimmery fulgent dome encompassed Qaasim. The sound of Seraphima's wings beat hard and swift when she veered away to avert a collision with the light field. She slowly descended and stood before Qaasim.

She inquisitively touched the protective field and it violently propelled her back, sending her crashing into the concrete wall of the underpass. Rocks and rubble fell to the ground from a cracked indention of her upper torso. She laid knocked out cold from unexpected impact.

Her energetic saber sword retracted itself and rolled about a foot away from her hand. Its handle was forged from polished iridium and covered in angelic symbols.

"Somebody pick it up," Keenan said.

Jaquan was the closest, so he quickly leaned down and grabbed it.

"Aaaahhhgg!" he screamed when it singed his hand.

Everyone jumped back and the saber rolled to the ground again.

Red removed Qaasim's shield and ran to Jaquan's aid, "Jaquan, you aight?"

He agonized in pain, "Aaaaahhh, it burns!"

"Let me see," she said.

Jaquan opened his hand and revealed a ghastly white burn that bubbled and smoked. Red reached into her bosoms and fetched her medicine bag. It was packed to the brim with thick, cold, and crumbly blood moon soil. She removed a few large pieces and spit on them until they moistened. Red spread the healing salve across Jaquan's wound. He exhaled with relief as his hand healed before his eyes, leaving a brown keloid scar.

"Somebodies' gotta pick it up. I remember reading about that sword. It's the only thing that can kill a seraphim," Raysean said as they all stood around Seraphima.

They all glanced around at each other for a volunteer.

"I definitely ain't touching it. Jaquan's hand looks like somebody shitted in it," Keenan joked.

"We can't kill her! She's just a child." Red said.

"Red's right. It's not her fault that she was probably programmed...sold a fantasy at The School of Understanding Self...just like many others...like myself. I mean look at her. I'll give her nine years old, at best. She still has an opportunity to grow and change her mind about things...we can't..."

They were all startled by Seraphima's face and foot wings simultaneously closing. Her powerful flying wings propelled her spinning upwards like a reverse twister. The suction of the mini cyclone lifted them off the ramp and dropped them back to the ground. Seraphima dove for her enormous angelic blade. Keenan used telekinesis to push the divine weapon away from her.

Her eyes shot in Keenan's direction.

"Keenan, don't look at her!" Raysean yelled.

It was too late. Seraphima and Keenan were locked in some sort of hypnotic gaze. Then, Seraphima opened her mouth and let out the most horrific sound. Its chord resounded like a ship's horn at sea.

Keenan began to levitate as Seraphima hovered closer and closer to him. Her voice boomed so great that the entire viaduct swayed and trembled. Cars driving above could be heard violently piling up. Seraphima and Keenan continued to float before each other in a mesmerized mystical state. Keenan's eyes began to glow a beautiful electric blue.

"Put him down right now!" Raysean screeched.

He stood clenching his eyes tightly with his feet shoulder length apart, wielding Seraphima's saber as if they were nunchucks. Raysean swung, swirled, and displayed thrusting skills that he did not remember learning. The giant mythical blade made whipping sounds as it sliced through the air.

Seraphima turned sharply in Raysean's direction and Keenan fell a few feet back down to the ground. Red rushed to his aid. His eyes changed back to their pure honey tone. In slight pain, he mumbled something unclear to her. She asked him to repeat it as Gator, Qaasim, and Jaquan squatted beside them.

"Slow down, Keenan. I can't understand you," Red said.

"It sounds like he's saying – Don't let him kill her!" Qaasim interpreted.

All of their heads swung in the direction of the impending clash. Raysean's senses were at their peaks. He stood on guard with Seraphima's angelic blade in his grips. Seraphima swooped down, scooped up her cloak, and teleported herself directly behind him.

Without turning, Raysean thrusted the blade between his waist and armpit.

The chef peered from inside of the pantry door. He turned and smiled at the housekeeper fixing her uniform behind him.

"The kitchen light's also out...probably just a fuse. Now, where were we?"

He dipped back into the pantry and pulled her in close to him. The sound of a pot falling to the floor startled them.

"Oh, no. It's the Senator! I can't lose my job," the housekeeper exclaimed.

"Just calm down. Be cool and he won't suspect a thing. I'll walk out first."

The housekeeper groveled in a corner next to a shelf with large bags of beans and rice when she heard loud commotion from outside of the pantry door. The sound of the chef's voice shrieked in between loud clinks and clanks. A pool of blood spilled from beneath the door.

The door slowly creaked when it opened. Bug-eyed and unable to see, the housekeeper shook in dread. She let out an ear-piercing squall after feeling Saada's whiskers tickling her face.

"Senator O'Conner," the Senator impatiently spoke into the receiver.

"Senator! Quick...you must come home!" Saada yelled.

"Rosetta, what is the problem?" he asked.

"It's the chef. There has been an accident," she sobbed.

"Accident? What happened?"

"We were in the kitchen...and...and...he started to touch me...and...and...I tried to make him stop...so I grabbed a knife...he wouldn't stop...!" she cried flustered.

"So, you murdered him in my kitchen?" he hollered.

"I couldn't make him stop!"

There was a long pause before the Senator responded.

"Have you told anyone else about it?"

"No, sir."

"Clean up, as best as you can. I'm on my way."

"Yes, sir."

Saada placed the phone back onto its base, adjusted her cleaning uniform, and strutted down a long hallway. She was proud of her Emmy worthy performance. Photos of the Senator taken with the current and former presidents, along with some famous people filled the walls. At the end of the hallway was a tall heavy locked door. She protracted a long claw-like nail from her index finger and picked the lock. The loud click bounced down the hall.

Saada turned the knob and walked inside.

Seraphima winced when she sat up. Her fingers coursed her cracked breastplate. She hugged herself and sighed, grateful that she had worn that heavy old thing. It absorbed all of the energy from the celestrial sword, the only object in the world powerful enough to kill her. She wondered how Raysean was even able to hold it. Only the most divine had to ability to clutch the Silver Saber.

Still a bit stunned, Seraphima slowly began to recall overhearing bits of the teens' debate on whether or not she should live or die. She couldn't believe that she had really come that close to dying. "There is a God, I guess," she exhaled sardonically.

Seraphima's eyes searched her immediate surroundings for the teens.

Before her, written in the dust on a steel metal beam, was a fingered message.

Dear Angel Girl,

Sorry that my cousin stabbed you. N – E - O ways...I hope u don't mind that we borrowed your sword...and ur really cool cloak. I'm sure we'll c u again real soon...so we promise to take good care of ur stuff.

C U later,

Keenan

Seraphima nervously glanced around for her tools. Her saber and teleportation cloak were gone. She sucked her teeth and pounded the pavement. Now, she would have to fly anywhere she needed to go. Seraphima hated to fly because, in order to keep her existence concealed, she was required to fly high - higher than the eye could see. Higher than the clouds, even. Teleportation was her preferred method of traveling, next to riding in a car. Staring out of the window, she would often imagine having the same freedoms as the vehicle that she was riding in. She so desperately yearned for the liberty to fly freely, without the fear of being reprimanded for being seen. Seraphima didn't understand why her existence was to remain a secret, when most religious people believed in angels anyways. She hovered to her feet when she heard tires screeching to a halt. It was the Senator and his driver. Senator O'Conner motioned for Seraphima to approach the vehicle. The wings on her feet fluttered at a high-velocity and closed a distance of approximately one hundred feet in mere a second.

She was relieved to see the SUV's door swing open, until she heard his thoughts. Hidden behind a faux grin and flushed cheeks was a very perturbed individual. Seraphima wanted so badly to initiate an orphic download of the Senator's memory. She settled, instead, for listening to his thoughts. Eye contact wasn't required in order to listen and it was much more discreet. The first thing that she noticed was that his thoughts did not align with his words.

There! There she is! There goes that incompetent little girl!

168

"Seraphima. Quick! Hop in! We followed your scream to this underpass."

Can't afford for any more goddamned videos to go viral! Do they even teach The Rules For Supernatural Engagement in Public Places, at the school anymore? Apparently, not. This girl is dumber than a box of damned rocks.

"Where's Qaasim and Jaquan?" the Senator asked in a slightly elevated tone.

Seraphima shrugged her shoulders and shut the door behind her. She hated to be yelled at and despised being condescended even more.

Hello? Are you just dumb or dumb and mute?

"Neither!" Seraphima fumed.

Senator O'Conner responded by sharing a confused expression with the driver through the rear view mirror. The driver glanced at Seraphima. She quickly made his eyes dart away by setting her eyes ablaze. If he had stared, but only a moment longer, she would've been privileged to all of the skeletons in his closet.

Are you reading my mind, Seraphima?

"Hhhmmph, maybe," she responded aloud.

"The school doesn't take lightly to its students using their gifts on authority."

"Well, you think too loud."

"Seraphima, I just watched a video of you flying. It showed you swooping down like you were going to pick something up. When you came back up, a fairly large young woman suddenly appeared in your grasps. That's when Qaasim and Jaquan seemed to pop out of thin air. They were captured on video fleeing across Louis Coleman Jr. Drive, barely evading traffic. And, the girl has already made a statement, which of course – has gone viral. Now, we have to send a very convincing retractor out to the hospital get her to remember things differently. It's imperative that you follow the rules!"

Seraphima rolled her eyes and stared out of the window.

"It's not like you mentioned that there would be five other people with him."

"Five other people? What do you mean, there were five other people?"

"There were five others – three boys, a nasty old man, and a girl. And, they all had their own special gifts, as well. They were clever enough to steal my sword and cloak. Who were they and how was the one that they called, Raysean, able to wield my angel sword without combusting?"

"Raysean and Keenan!" Senator O'Conner grumbled to himself.

"So, you know them, huh?"

Why am I not surprised?

"Who were the others? Were they gifted as well?"

"Were they gifted? Raysean not only handled my sword with expert precision, but he did it with his eyes closed, so that I couldn't terrify him to death! The girl, she was able to command birds, heal, and cast shields with just her voice. I ran into one and knocked myself out cold. I'm not stupid. Abilities like that require spells and the assistance of divine beings like myself. And then, the old man – he was a dead man walking with a lot of strength. You basically sent me on a suicide mission."

Damn it! It's happening. Their gifts are getting stronger and they've already begun attracting others to themselves. I have to find them before the prophecy is fulfilled!

"What about the other two boys?" he asked.

She hesitated, "Oh, they didn't give me much of a fight," she lied. Her mind shifted to Keenan. Seraphima had never been attracted to anyone in her life, and there she was protecting him. She had intended for him to be another notch on her forearm, but instead, she wondered if she would be just another under his belt.

On the outside looking in, their encounter lasted less than a minute. But, to Seraphima and Keenan it was the equivalent to an entire day. Upon psychic impact, Keenan did something unusual. Instead of cringing in fear, he opened up more to her. He revealed to her that the demon that she attempted to frighten him with, often stalked him as a kid. Keenan also shared with her his triumph over the malevolent entity. He had psychically taken her to the same peaceful place where he saw Lotus prostrating on across the cove. Seraphima opened up to him as well, feeling totally free to be transparent, as well. When she shared that she was an atheist, Keenan didn't bat an eye. He didn't pass judgment, nor did he crack a joke. Instead, he gazed into her eyes and asked her if she believed in him.

"Of course, you're standing right here," she answered plainly.

"So, basically God'll have to stand right in front of you before you'll believe?"

"I've interacted with spirits, heard the prayers of healers and saints, and have smited demons with my sword and *God* has remained invisible through it all."

Keenan stared out at the cove. His dimples adorned a peaceful smile.

"This may sound crazy," he said, "but I think that we're all God. No words had ever ringed so true to her.

They talked and skipped rocks across the still waters until she heard Raysean commanding her to put Keenan back down on the ground. But, it wasn't her that had Keenan suspended in mid-air. He was levitating. Seraphima remembered feeling in those moments where time stood still, as if she was a part of him. It was the only time in her life where she didn't feel completely alone. Keenan was like a crackle to her inner flame.

"Seraphima!" the Senator yelled.

She snapped out of her daydream.

"Did they mention where they were going?"

Yes, to your house.

"No," she fibbed again.

She didn't trust his motives and wanted to be the first to find
them.

"Well, I need to make a quick detour to my home. There's been a
bit of an emergency."

Gator and the teens all appeared out of thin air, huddling under
Seraphima's enormous cloak. They looked as if they were trying
to shield themselves from an impending downpour.

"I think that we're here," Raysean said.

Qaasim peeked from beneath the heavy cloth. He couldn't see
his hand before his face. They were in total darkness. He was
relieved to feel the soothing feeling of his cat brushing in
between his ankles.

"Yes, we are here," Qaasim rejoiced, "and I never thought I'd be
so happy!"

"Why's it so dark, man? I can't see shit," Jaquan asked.

"Lights," Qaasim spoke aloud.

Nothing happened.

"Itaka, what's with you? Turn on the lights," he commanded his
super computer.

Raysean applied pressure to the inside of his palms and they
shone bright like flashlights. He located a light switch, walked
over and flipped it. Nothing happened. Raysean flipped it up
and down vigorously.

"No power," he said.

"No worries. The Senator does this from time to time when he
tries to discipline me. He knows that programming is my life, so
he cuts the power to my room. What he doesn't know is that I
installed a voice operated backup generator inside of Itaka. So,
when he cuts my power for days – I'm really on a mini vacation
inside of my room," he gloated.

"Back-up generator on!"

The lights came on and revealed a bedroom that a geek would
die for. On one wall, six one hundred and ten inch television

screens came to life. They all displayed the same screensaver, Qaasim's name bouncing around each one. A handsome black sectional with enormous ottomans formed a cozy cul de sac. Exclusive and vintage gaming systems were housed on display in a glass case nearby.

At the far end of the room was a bed fit for a king. It was posh with a masculine appeal and opened up to a spacious walk-in bathroom that beckoned them all. It had tempered glass and was encased by polished black and grey marble tiles that gleamed beneath dimmed tray lights.

A life-sized replica of the Black Panther comic book character stood with his arms crossed as if on guard. Its muscles bulged and veins sprawled through an all black fully protective bodysuit. A heavy black cape draped around its shoulders and hung at its feet.

It stood before a wall that opened up into a tremendous walk-in closet. Synchronized by color, were rows and rows of custom made Italian designer suits with the accessories to match.

And, then there was the hidden kitchen. It was concealed behind a black paneled wall and was fully equipped with the most contemporary appliances.

"Welcome home, Qaasim," a feminine voice spoke through the surround sound.

"It's good to be home, Itaka. It's been a very eventful day. I see that the Senator cut our power again. Sorry that I was away so long."

"The power was not cut by Senator O'Conner this time. This time, it was cut by an unknown source located on this property, sir."

Everyone's eyes met each other's. They knew that they didn't have long before they would possibly have to fend for their lives again. Raysean broke the silence.

"Why'd you insist on bringing us here – to the home of a man that you say wants to kill us? This better be good." he interrogated.

All eyes were on Qaasim. He cut right to the chase.

"Itaka, show them what we discovered," he spoke.

Like magic, luminescent holographic screens and networks surrounded them and every inch of the room. The space in which they all stood radiated a luminous violet glow. They were amazed by what they witnessed, as they stood amidst a virtual computer lab.

Itaka manipulated the screens until she came across a top-secret document. She flipped through the pages until they all saw the words "Dark Skies" typed in a tiny font. They were the only words on the first page of the document. Itaka turned the page. The next page was the exact opposite. It was full of words, short and long ones. Raysean became anxious.

"Look man, we didn't come here to read no essays. You said that you had some important information to share with us...so spit!"

"You're right. We don't know how much time we have before we're discovered again, so I'll get right to it. When's the last time you looked up at the sky?"

Keenan burst into laughter, "Aw shit, this nigga bout' to kick some poetry?"

"Aw, man. Here we go..." Jaquan sighed placing his hand on his forehead.

"Nigga? Nigga? Do you know what the definition of a nigger is?" Qaasim beseeched.

"Yea...you nigga." Keenan pressed back.

Qaasim's eyes ricocheted around their circle. He had anticipated some competition from Keenan, but nothing as aggressive as what he encountered. Qaasim felt his temperature rising. Being called a nigger or nigga was the equivalent of being called a kaffir, a derogatory term used against Africans. There was no word more offensive to him. The word "nigga" nearly brought him and Jaquan to blows twice.

"While your ummi was getting you dressed each morning for preschool, I was flying in military jets to Alaska to program a machine that can control the weather. So, while you were just learning your ABC's and making mud pies, I was creating mudslides and making it rain on Southern California. For your information, Keenan, the definition of a nigger is an ignorant person. I don't see any niggers in this room, do you?" he retorted.

Keenan's eyes darted towards Red when he heard her snicker, then he stepped towards Qaasim. Raysean intervened, ending the fight before it could begin.

"Both of ya'll some dumb niggas...if you think I came here to waste my time!"

"Raysean's right, ya'll. Any moment now, *God knows what* could come crashing through that door!" Red agreed as she shifted from side to side.

Keenan and Qaasim ended their stare down.

"Itaka, track the Senator. Where is his vehicle now?" Qaasim inquired.

"I have located his vehicle traveling at 90 miles an hour on I64 heading eastbound. It appears that he is headed home. At the speed that he is traveling, he is expected to arrive here in approximately thirty seven minutes and fourteen seconds."

"And, we need to be long gone by then," Keenan protested.

"Well, if you'd let me finish, then we could very well have already been on our way."

"So, you're going with us?" Red asked Qaasim with excitement in her voice.

"I can't stay here. I'm an asset that's already defected. That already makes me a traitor in The Agency's eyes. As far as they're concerned, I have already told you everything that I know. Traitors are always marked for death, regardless of age, sex, or abilities."

"The Agency?" Raysean echoed.

"Yes. Years ago, I discovered that the Senator is one of many pawns that work for The Brotherhood. It's a vile, purebred family that uses The Agency to carry out its agendas. The Agency is made up of individuals strategically placed in corporations, organizations, schools, universities, medical institutions, law enforcement, legal institutions, correctional facilities, political arenas, media groups, and especially in science. They're everywhere, man. And, we'll have to stick together from here on out, in order to have a true chance at survival...now the reason that I asked you all when you looked up at the sky last was, because World War III has taken place and the world doesn't even know it. Sure, the subject of climate change is tossed up in the air here and there, but there have not been any serious discussions or debates about it – except for on conspiracy websites or YouTube videos. But, if you look up - high up in the sky, you'll see unmanned planes that leave zigzag white lines that thicken, spread, and create artificial clouds. Inside of the chemical sprays are infinite metal particles that are breathed in or absorbed through the skin and create illness and death in many cases. It's very much like slow euthanasia. The metal particles are also used in conjunction with a very powerful magnet to create catastrophic natural disasters such as Hurricane Katrina, the earthquake in Haiti, and the tsunami in Japan. I know, because I was the programmer on these projects."

Qaasim looked away with great regret when he heard Red gasp.

"We all done shit we ain't proud of, Qaasim," Jaquan asserted.

"But, what does all of this have to do with us?" Keenan asked impatiently.

"It's about population control. Out with the original human race and in with GMH's – Genetically Modified Humans. Millions of GMH's already exist around the world. They are either born

176

naturally from people that have consumed genetically modified organisms, or artificially - like the angel girl was more than likely created. GMH's don't usually have abilities. They are mostly docile humans easily programmed to be nothing more than economic or industrial slaves. They are easily distracted and influenced. But, peppered into this soup of sick people are anomalies."

Qaasim looked around at them all...you...him...her...him...me...the girl, Ashley...and there's another that I know of...a girl named Lotus...we're all..."

Raysean interrupted Qaasim in the middle of his speech.

"Lotus? How do you know Lotus? Do you know where she is?" Raysean asked with Qaasim's shirt balled tight in his grips.

The group shuffled around until they separated the two. Qaasim readjusted his dress shirt and cautiously proceeded where he left off.

"We're all what The Agency calls *super psychics*. And Lotus, well I remember her from The School of Understanding Self. It was very clear that she was different from us others. She was not a student, but instead, a very powerful master teacher. I had not seen her nor heard her name spoken of since our flight to the states...that is until I saw her face on the news the other day when she was kidnapped from your school. It was the same day that I overheard the Senator say your names – Raysean and Keenan. In a hacked conference call with The Agency, I heard them tell him to find you two before Saada found you and reunited you *again*. Their fear was that your union could awaken the dormant abilities in thousands – possibly millions of children that have yet to be affected by their toxic cocktail sprays. When I overheard the Senator's phone call giving the governor instructions to pardon your father from prison, as well as, the call to the funeral home to pay for your services, I knew there had to be more to all of this. The Senator doesn't have a compassionate bone in his body. All of his donations are investments. So, I hit up Jaquan to ask him how well he knew you. Then, down the rabbit hole we went and here we all stand. Well, that's the nutshell version of it anyways."

"So, this chick Saada don't work for the Senator?" Raysean asked.

"That *chick* Saada don't work for no one! She's rogue and she's a pain in the ass to The Agency. I think that she's pretty cool actually – especially being that she shifts into a black panther."

"So, she's not a killer?" Keenan asked for assurance.

"*Now*, I didn't say that. I'm just saying that I like the fact that she's a loner and has no problem holding her own that's all."

"Well, Ray – looks like your girlfriend may still be alive," Keenan poked.

Raysean rolled his eyes, "Do you know how we can find Saada?"

Qaasim laughed, "Find Saada? You don't find Saada. Saada finds you. And, once she has your scent, there's no escaping her."

"Saada, you got company. Five hot bodies on the third floor, east end of the house. They just appeared from out of nowhere. I'm on my way," said Nadia.

Saada was copying all of the files from Senator O'Connor's computer. She wanted to investigate what Nadia saw, but the download was so close to completion. With her head slightly tilted back, she sniffed the air.

"Hhhmmmpphh," she smiled and stared at the ceiling.

"They're here! Allahu Akbar! This is too damned good to be true."

Senator O'Conner, the driver, and Seraphima entered the dark foyer. The Senator flipped the light switch. Then again and again, "Rosetta!" he called out to his housekeeper.

Saada's head shot up from the computer screen and then back down.

The download was at ninety seven percent.

"Come on! Come on!" she sibilated.

"Rosetta! Where are you? What happened to the power?"
Senator O'Conner removed the gun that was hidden on his ankle, the driver clutched his automatic weapon tighter, and then they proceeded with extreme caution. The driver bumped into an expensive vase. It wobbled wildly and nearly toppled over.
The lights suddenly came back on and standing before them was Saada wearing Rosetta's body. She wore a risqué maid uniform with bloodstained thigh high stockings that were held up by a salacious lace garter.
The Senator took one look at her and felt the urge to take her right then and there.
"Seraphima, could you give us a few moments alone? There's an urgent matter that I need to attend to. My son, Qaasim's room is on the third floor - the entire floor. Here...take the elevator. See if you can find anything that can lead us to his whereabouts."
Seraphima nodded and stepped into the elevation box. The doors closed and she immediately began to smile. She knew that Qaasim and the others were upstairs, because she could feel the call of her stolen celestial devices intensifying as she neared.
The cry sounded like a dramatic orchestra of crystal singing bowls.
The number three button glowed brightly and then there was a soft ding. Seraphima stepped off the elevator when the doors opened. Her protracted angel sword and teleportation cloak were suspended and awaiting her in the air. She sheathed her sword and tossed the heavy cloak around her shoulders like a matador champion.
The room appeared to be empty, but their head chatter gave them all away.
"You may as well show yourselves. I know that you're here, because I can hear your thoughts."
Seraphima used telekinetic energy to open the wall and revealed the hidden kitchen that they were all hiding inside of.

"You thieves have five seconds to convince me why I shouldn't release devil dogs from hell upon you!" Seraphima threatened them with her hands on her hips.

Everyone stood up from their hiding places, but Keenan was the only one that stepped forward.

"Because, you're curious." Keenan spoke up.

His peek-a-boo dimples played hide-and-seek with her captivated gaze. She momentarily reminisced on the evening that they shared together at the cove during their trance. Seraphima was more than curious, she was pleasantly intrigued.

"Being that we've exceeded five seconds, is it safe to assume that our man, Keenan, here is correct in his assumptions?" Qaasim inquired.

"Maybe, a little," Seraphima unwillingly admitted.

She continued, "Like, how is it that you all are in tune with your abilities without attending a school like The School of US?

"I attended The School of US ten years ago. My friends are still enrolled and haven't been adopted by a suitable family yet – which is a fairytale, by the way. They refuse to believe me when I tell them that there is no such thing as a suitable family, or family period for that matter. We all get blinded by the glitz and glam of it all, but all that glitters, isn't gold."

Seraphima used her foot wings to zip around the room rapidly. She completed her tour of Qaasim's bedroom in only a few seconds. When she was back in the place she had started, she performed a three hundred sixty degree whirl then rebutted.

"It looks like you're doing pretty good to me."

"Looks are very deceiving. I can guarantee you that nothing you see here was worth the atrocities committed in order to acquire it. The adoption life isn't what the school makes it out to be! Our adoptions are actually business transactions between The Agency and the super rich. I hate to burst your bubble. But, there are no happily ever afters. No lights at the end of tunnels,

180

and no pots at the end of rainbows. All they do is use you."
Qaasim admitted with great disdain.

Seraphima's heart sank. She was speechless. She didn't know how to respond to a possibility that she had never even considered before. Adoption was a shared fantasy of all of the students at The School of US. And while, Seraphima knew that twelve years old was considered an old age for adoption, she still had her hopes. Qaasim's capture was the only thing that could seal the deal and Seraphima was determined to fulfill her conditional task.

The foundation shook them off of their feet when they heard and felt a loud crash.

"I'm sorry, but I need you to come with me," Seraphima said hovering above Qaasim.

She swooped down, covered him with her cloak, and in a blink of an eye, they were gone.

Gator and the teens clambered to their feet.

"Oh, shit! She took him," Jaquan exclaimed.

Gator helped Red back onto her feet, "What the heck was that?" she asked.

"The source of the crash was a Chevrolet Camaro driving through the front door," Itaka answered.

"Chevy Camaro?" Keenan asked.

"What color is it and how many doors does it have?" Raysean inquired.

"The color is black...number of doors...four." Itaka's voice resounded.

"It's Saada. If we find Saada, we find Lotus." Raysean spoke undoubtedly.

"And, what about Qaasim?" Red asked.

"What about him?" Raysean responded.

"Is your plan to just forget about him?" She pressed.

"I ain't tryna be smart or nothing by saying this, but didn't you just see the angel girl take him like it was nothing? You do realize that we just used her coat to bring us here, right? That means that they could be anywhere in the world right now! How do you expect us to find a needle in a haystack?" Keenan chimed in.

"Qaasim is currently being held by his captor on the first floor, where a lurid altercation is taking place. He desperately needs your help." Itaka answered again.

The group glanced around at one another in search for signs of agreement.

Raysean walked over to the elevator and pushed the button marked for down. The doors opened and he stepped inside. Jaquan sighed and joined him. Red and Gator were next, leaving Keenan standing in limbo.

"Cuz, I read somewhere that if we don't stand for something, we'll fall for anything. You heard Qaasim when he said, 'Saada finds you.' Do you really wanna spend the rest of your life running from this woman? I don't!"

Keenan reluctantly stepped inside of the elevator and pushed number one. He turned when he felt Red's soft palm caress him from the top to the small of his back. She greeted him with a smile of approval. Her hand was warm and comforting. It was the encouragement that he needed to exit those doors when they finally popped open. The two-floor journey felt like an eternity. Keenan was the first to exit against a hail of bullets. He quickly ducked back inside, barely escaping harm. A black blur fled past the elevator doors. Everyone inside nearly jumped out of their skins.

"What the hell was that? It was big ass fuck!" Jaquan cried.

"That was Saada! Red, do that force field thing that you did again under the viaduct. Then, we're all going to walk out together." Raysean quickly strategized.

"Shield!" Red called out.

A translucent dome surrounded them when they stepped out of the elevator all huddled together. Bullets bounced off of the protective field as they scanned their surroundings. Saada was spotted crouching behind a wall. She hissed in the direction of the gunfire. The hellfire momentarily stopped. The sound of car doors slamming and rapid footsteps replaced the rain of hot metal pellets.

"Come on out, Saada. There's nowhere to run. The house is surrounded by agents. But, you still have a choice. Give us Lotus and the kuten Qi and I'll give you your estranged son," the Senator shouted.

Saada gnashed her teeth and arched her back as she anamorphed back into her human form. Her long dreadlocks wrapped wildly and clung to her body giving her full coverage of her intimate places. She yelled from behind the wall that she hid.

"Like I told you before, The Original Gods don't negotiate with terrorists. I have another plan. Let my son go, or the videos that I found on your computer of you molesting those little Cambodian girls go public. You sick bastard!"

A devious laugh spilled from the Senator's thin lips and filled the room.

"When you're as rich and powerful as I am, you're entitled to your delicacies."

"Listen to him! You hear that? He's a predator! You should let me go now, before it's too late for us all." Qaasim pleaded with Seraphima.

"Be still! You're not the only one that deserves a chance at living a normal life!" Seraphima said with her arm around his neck and her sword inches from his back.

"Speaking of delicacies. I can smell the reptilian blood flowing through your veins. It's been sometime since I've had lizard meat. It is certainly an acquired taste." Saada said as she growled a cat-like jape.

"I haven't eaten all day. I saved my appetite just for you," she added.

"Seraphima, quick! Bring Qaasim to me." The Senator commanded.

Seraphima draped Qaasim up in her cloak and teleported to the Senator's side.

"What now? How do we get Qaasim without leaving this shield?" Jaquan asked.

They all surveyed the room as they peered from inside of the protective sphere.

The Senator grabbed Qaasim by the bicep with crushing strength and jerked him over to him. Qaasim struggled with all his might, but he was no match for the transmutable Senator. A long slitted tongue slivered from his mouth and across Qaasim's face. He yanked his face away when he smelled Senator O'Conner's pungent breath. A smoky green mist that slowly dissipated accompanied the foul odor.

"Let me go! You could kill me with your breath alone!" Qaasim protested.

A jagged elongated tail protruded from the Senator's backside and ripped through his tailored suit. He released Qaasim from his grasps and then used his powerful tail to suspend Qaasim up in the air by his neck. The Senator terrorized Qaasim with his venomous fangs. They oozed a gooey lime colored substance. Qaasim's arms and legs flung out wildly. His eyes pleaded for help.

"One bite and your son will be nothing more than a memory." The Senator warned.

Saada peeked around the corner and saw the fully shifted Senator dangling Qaasim by the throat. His face was as purple as a plum. Saada fell back against the wall that she hid behind. She banged the back of head on it for having too much pride to ask Lucus for help when she called him earlier. Saada began to hyperventilate as tears fell from her eyes.

"Sssshhhh. Don't cry, Saada." Nadia spoke into Saada's embedded earpiece.

Then, she began to rev her engine. Seraphima teleported herself beside the vehicle. She placed one hand on the passenger side door and looked inside. The four door Camaro was completely empty.

Instantly, Seraphima's eyes rolled into the back of her head and she felt herself take a passenger seat in her own body. Wearing Seraphima's avatar, Nadia spun upwards, as high up as she could go. She opened her mouth and released the most awful sound. Everything fragile object within ear range, was heard crashing to hard surfaces. Then, out of nowhere, two massive three headed devil dogs appeared on the ground beneath her. They gnarled and gnashed their teeth at the Senator and his driver as Nadia held their energetic leashes tightly. Their eyes glowed like burning cinders and from their mouths seeped steamy smoke. "Seraphima! What the hell are you doing?" The Senator screamed.

"Let my nephew go!" Nadia demanded.

"Your nephew? Is that you, Nadia? Wow! This day has just been full of surprises," said the Senator.

Qaasim slammed his head on the floor when Senator O'Conner threw him down like a toddler that tosses a toy that he or she is no longer interested in.

"But, how? It was me that gave the order for the sniper to unleash the bullet that barrowed through your skull during your little rebellion! I saw you die, Nadia!"

The Senator hocked and spit a venomous loogie at her. She dodged it by beating Seraphima's wings swiftly. Acid venom hit the chandelier, making it rain Swarovski crystals.

Red released the shield and rushed to Qaasim's aid. Saada was right on her heels. She pushed Red out of the way and fell on top of Qaasim. Cradling his limp head in her bosoms, Saada cried out louder than she had the night she'd given birth to him. Nadia unleashed hells hounds upon the Senator and the driver. They opened their mouths and flames shot out like flamethrowers.

185

The Senator turned his back and swung his powerful tail, knocking the demon dogs across the room. The driver ducked behind a grand piano and called for backup through a radio on his wrist.

"What the hell are you waiting for...a God damned invitation? Get the hell in here and bring everything that you got!"

Agents with concealed faces and dressed in all black, filed inside by the dozen with their weapons drawn. A series of clicks from their military issued artillery being cocked, echoed throughout the room.

"Don't move!" An agent shouted.

"Wait! Hands up! Don't shoot!" Jaquan cried out when he raised his hands.

One agent fired, then the rest followed suit. The blasts from their weapons sounded like rapid thunder. Raysean, Keenan, and Gator ducked, rolled, and dove across the floor until they found refuge back inside of the elevator. Bullet spray pelted the heavy metal that encased it. Raysean instantly checked himself for injury.

"You aight?" He asked Keenan panting.

"Yea. I think so. We gotta get the fuck out of here, bruh!" Keenan said out of breath.

Raysean turned to the wall and air drew the invisible door sigil. It hovered and shone brilliantly.

"What's out there this time?" Keenan asked as his chest heaved in and out.

Raysean cautiously reached his arm through the ancient floating symbol and something snatched him through to the other side. His sneakers made squeaking sounds against the tiled flooring when he tried to resist. Keenan jumped up to his rescue, but another hail of gunfire pelted the elevator again. He and Gator ducked into the corner.

"Stop! Stop! Don't shoot!" Keenan screamed from the pits of his stomach.

186

The gunfire stopped.

"Jaquan!" Keenan shouted.

There was no answer.

"Red!" he called out again.

All he could hear was Saada sobbing relentlessly. Keenan activated his telekinesis with all of his might and then walked out of the elevator. Sporadic gunfire started again, but ended quickly when the force of the energy exuding from Keenan's palms sent the agents flying back through the door, windows, and into the wall. Keenan heard what sounded like a base drum beating above his head. He looked up and Nadia gave him a nod of approval just before she swooped down to Saada and Qaasim's aid.

"Red! Red! We gotta go!" Keenan said shaking her by the shoulders.

Her hands were cupped around her mouth and tears streamed down her face. She was in shock with her eyes locked on Jaquan. He lay mangled and bloody amidst shards of glass, empty bullet shells, and chunks of drywall.

Nadia squatted down, closed her eyes, and caressed Qaasim's forehead. His eyes popped open and then he shoved Saada away when he found himself in her arms. Qaasim staggered to his feet and looked around. He was completely discombobulated and had no memory of anything that happened after Seraphima kidnapped him from his room. Qaasim's eyes searched around wildly at all of the carnage.

Agents lay sprawled out across the floor. The two devils dogs lay whining as they bled out. And then, his eyes fell on Jaquan's motionless body lying on the ground. He gasped at the sight of his best friend's lifeless body. Qaasim's bloodshot eyes targeted Saada.

"What did you do to him?" Qaasim screamed as he charged her.

He stopped just short of lunging at her throat when he began choking himself. Qaasim gagged as he struggled against his own might.

Keenan continued to tug on Red until she finally looked into his eyes. Hers finally mirrored the same sense of urgency as his.

"We gotta go, Red! We gotta find Raysean! Something pulled him through the invisible door!" He exclaimed.

She hesitated when she saw Qaasim choking himself.

Saada said to herself, "There's only one person that I know of that can make a person try to kill themselves. No, Lucus! No!" she yelled pelting Qaasim in the chest.

A phantom-like figure released Qaasim, and then stepped out of his shadow. Qaasim stumbled backwards grateful to be breathing again.

"Come on, man! Let's go!" Keenan shouted as he did a reverse skip.

Qaasim grabbed Red by the hand and they ran with Keenan towards the elevator.

They were nearly blinded by bright flashes that accompanied loud booms. Thick smoke quickly began to fill the room.

"Run, son! Run!" Saada shouted from behind them.

Qaasim looked back with a confused expression on his face just before they all disappeared inside of the elevator. Before Saada, Nadia, and Lucus could pursue them, they heard popping sounds. They turned to see a pair of electromagnetic nets being launched in their direction. Nadia threw Seraphima's cloak around Saada, and in a blink of an eye, they were gone. Lucus wasn't so lucky. One of the nets captured him sending just enough electricity through his body to stun him, but not enough to allow Lucus to manifest his physical body. Lucus collapsed to the floor. The electromagnetic shocks coursed through his body, enslaving him to the ground.

"Well...well...what do we have here?" The Senator taunted.

"Could it really be the mystical shadow walker, Lucus, in the flesh?" He jeered.

Lucus flinched from every shock.

Senator O'Conner motioned with his head for some agents to check the elevator. They walked over to the elevator with their guns drawn.

"It's empty, sir," one of them turned and reported.

"What did you just say?" The Senator asked for clarification purposes.

"I said – it's empty, sir!" The agent repeated.

"F-UUUUUUUUUCK!" Senator O'Conner yelled.

Cheketa Tinsley

Cheketa Tinsley is an entrepreneur, Reiki Master, and metaphysicist. Prior to business ownership, she had a corporate career in accounting and purchasing. With child and family advocacy at her core, Cheketa was honored at the fourth annual Saturday Academy Sistah Summit hosted by the University of Louisville's College of Arts and Sciences for her work to inspire black women. When she's not writing, Cheketa is a Life *Purpose* Coach and uses unconventional sciences, such as, astrology and numerology as guides. She has two shape-shifting daughters and four magical grandsons - and resides in Louisville, Kentucky with her energy wielding husband, and three wild beasts. You can visit her at www.CheketaTinsley.com.

Sooooooo...what do you think?

I would love to hear from you and promise to respond to every post with #cheketatinsley in it. Below are other hashtags that I use often. I invite you to utilize them as well.

I need your help getting this book out there to the world, therefore, I encourage you to follow Strange Clouds, share any posts that resonate with you, and/or create a group(s) to start your own book discussion(s) around it.

#strangeclouds #strangecloudstheseries #502comeup #melanatedfantasy #fanmel #superheroes #psychicabilities #environmentaljustice #racialjustice #economicjustice #chemtrails #thoseaintnoclouds #geoengineering #saynotogmo #rebelswithacause #raysean #keenan #lotus #auntieqi #red #gator #saada #nadia #lucus #senatoroconner #seraphima #qaasim #hatinassjaquan #theschoolofus #telepaths #mediums #shapeshifters #goddesses #zombies #lizardpeople #channeling #healing #sage #voodou #possessiveteleportation #shadowwalker #photographiccellmemory #leadersofthenewschool #theoriginalgods #theogs #highlyaddicttivefantasy #blackfantasy #uncensoredstorytelling #literaryclapback

For more info, backstories, and other strange morsels visit:

www.strangecloudstheseries.com

facebook/strangecloudsky

twitter/strangeclouds32

instagram/strangeclouds502

Made in the USA
Middletown, DE
27 May 2017